The Train to Paris

SEBASTIAN HAMPSON was born in 1992 in Auckland, New Zealand. He grew up in Wellington, has lived in Europe, and is currently studying art history and literature at Victoria University. *The Train to Paris* is his first novel.

The Train to Paris

Sebastian Hampson

TEXT PUBLISHING MELBOURNE AUSTRALIA

textpublishing.com.au

The Text Publishing Company
Swann House
22 William Street
Melbourne Victoria 3000 Australia

First published in 2014 by The Text Publishing Company
Reprinted 2014

Cover and page design by WH Chong
Typeset by J&M Typesetting

Printed in Australia by Griffin Press, an Accredited ISO AS/NZS 14001:2004 Environmental Management System printer.

National Library of Australia Cataloguing-in-Publication entry
Author: Hampson, Sebastian
Title: The Train to Paris / by Sebastian Hampson.
ISBN: 9781922147790 (paperback)
ISBN: 9781922148780 (ebook)
Subjects: Love stories.
Voyages and travel—Fiction.
Dewey Number: A823.4

This book is printed on paper certified against the Forest Stewardship Council® Standards. Griffin Press holds FSC chain-of-custody certification SGS-COC-005088. FSC promotes environmentally responsible, socially beneficial and economically viable management of the world's forests.

This project has been assisted by the Commonwealth Government through the Australia Council, its arts funding and advisory body.

To my brother Rafe Hampson

Part I

1

Five hours and fifty-one minutes after my departure
I arrived at the border. It was a Friday afternoon at the end
of August and things could have been worse. Most people
would admire the charming Basque town of Hendaye, with
its sunbaked terraces and terracotta roofs, and I wanted to
be most people. I wanted to describe the idyllic scene before
me even though I could not see it clearly. The town drifted
into view from beyond a mess of overhead wires and signal
boxes, and I was so preoccupied by the matter at hand that
only a few details remain with me. Pastel-coloured buildings
cascaded down to the waterfront, while the shuttered villas
that stood on the bluff were the vestiges of wealth long
since spent. Hendaye was out of kilter and I had no desire
to linger there.

The train pulled in on the Spanish side of the station,
which was barricaded from the French by a wire fence.

This seemed a strange precaution when the French did not bother with passport control. I suspected it was more psychological than practical, a reminder that we were all crossing into unfamiliar territory.

I was among the first off the train. I made straight for the ticket office, along with two women whom I presumed were in the same strife. My ticket took me no further than the end of the Spanish line. The women must have noticed my panic—one of them asked if I was going to Paris. 'I hope so,' I said.

Both women had tans. I wondered where they might have acquired them. Certainly not Madrid. Nobody wanted to go to Madrid at this time of the year. I imagined they had taken a hotel in one of those purpose-built Mediterranean resort towns I had seen in advertisements.

Queuing—practically a way of life in this part of the world—gave me a chance to take in the surroundings. The station was bare and not exactly clean. Monet would have brushed over the finer points and left a hazy concourse filled with faceless people, but Daumier would have seen more: a paper napkin sliding across the ground in a draft, catching under the hard wooden benches that were cordoned off and labelled, *Transit Area*.

It was the dankest part of the station and I had to wonder why any transit passenger would choose to sit there. I knew very little about this station, or the town of

Hendaye for that matter, except that this was where Hitler, Franco and von Ribbentrop had met. That was appropriate enough.

The day was mild because of the raw, steely breeze that rolled in from the Atlantic. It was a relief from the scorched plains of Madrid, but it was still too sunny for my liking.

The displaced Parisians had made it to a ticket officer. I could not understand the conversation, which was in Spanish, but it was heated. This filled me with dread. After they left empty-handed I made my trepidatious way forward. He was my mental image of a ticket officer—small and portly, with round spectacles and thinning grey hair. He had the usual air of impatience, as though my allotted time with him was the greatest privilege I could hope for.

'Yes?' he said.

'Yes, hello. I need a ticket to Paris.'

'Paris? Today?'

'Yes.'

'No more to Paris this weekend.' I must have shown my confusion because he added an exasperated 'Full' in English, complete with a hand gesture. I was conscious of my perspiring brow.

'Is there nothing for the whole weekend?'

He motioned for the next in line to come forward. It was the end of the summer holidays. I should have known that every last Frenchman would want to go to Paris this weekend. How out of touch I was with the French timetable.

The departure board indicated that the next train to Paris was leaving in a quarter of an hour. It would have taken me there in time for a twilight drink at a café on the Boulevard Saint-Germain. The next and last train for the day was not due for another two hours—that, I presumed, was also full.

There was nothing to be done, so I waited in the station hall with my fellow travellers, all of whom appeared as lost as I felt. There were no derelicts. This was not Paris, I reminded myself, where I had heard the homeless were routinely rounded up and dropped in the countryside. Nonetheless I held my luggage close. One bag contained my laptop and my travel documents—whatever use they were—and the other was a slim and sensible trolley case. I was twenty years old, but I might have been a Parisian financier on holiday.

The queue was not dwindling, and it was awkward to stand at the front of the concourse, as if on a stage. Everything around me was in motion. I went over to the ticket machine, thinking that it might be more helpful than the officer. I set about trying to operate it, despite my bad French and worse Spanish. A regional train to Dax was departing soon, and I considered catching it. Dax was at least a familiar name. I waved down an assistant who was heading for the station offices, and asked him if this place had an internet connection anywhere. He did not understand me, and he could do nothing more than direct me back to the ticket officer, despite my insistences that he was not helping me either.

I walked aimlessly into the station's atrium, a brutal glass addition to the original neoclassical building. I could see the high-speed train to Paris from my new vantage point. The concourse was emptying around me, and soon I counted only a few other people. I watched as the carriages slid out of view to reveal the Dax train at the opposite platform. I could go there. It was better to go somewhere than nowhere. But something told me it would also be better to stay in this inhospitable wasteland. I felt sure that something would turn up.

She entered the station, wearing a white leopard-print dress that was short enough to show off her legs. Her hair slid down the back of her neck in a curtain of gold, which shimmered as it passed through the updraft. There was a conspicuous ring on her finger.

I allowed my gaze to linger as she crossed the concourse, trailing a designer suitcase. Her heels reverberated with each step. She was thin and her muscles were lean, yet the dress fit tight and her thighs pressed against the folds. She joined the queue in the ticket office and lit up a cigarette, puffing out smoke as though it meant nothing to her. I imagined that she was used to standing before a camera. She removed a pair of butterfly sun-glasses and hooked them into the neck of her dress. Her head turned and her eyes almost met with mine. I looked away.

A man sat next to me, so laden with luggage that he could have been creating a fortress around himself. His face was craggy and grey, and I felt him watching me. I pretended to busy myself, searching through travel documents for a non-existent answer to my problems. A fly landed on my arm and I flicked it away. My body was craving both coffee and water. There was no vending machine, no source of drink in this hellish building. But there was a photo booth. At least I would be able to take a pass-port photo, even if I died of dehydration.

Her confrontation with the balding ticket officer was also becoming heated. She was not the sort of person used to being denied. I saw her turn in profile as the officer did his best to explain himself. Now she was applying reason, having already shouted and implored.

The afternoon was young. I had time to go and explore the town. But above all else I needed a coffee. There was a café across the road from the station, with plastic chairs that looked as though they might collapse if anyone sat on them. The language of this region frustrated me—it was stuck somewhere between French and Spanish, but retained its own eccentric nuances. Seeing the name *Casa*

Miguel printed next to *Brasserie* increased my disorientation. Casa Miguel was the place to be in this town: two people were at the bar. Every other shop was shuttered away from the heat.

I took a table by the window and ordered a *café crème*. In Paris they would disapprove of the use of such peasant-like terms, but here it was the right thing to do.

She had followed me out of the station and now crossed the road, treating the flaky white lines like a catwalk. Her stride was all confidence. I watched as she drew near. She could see me, but pretended not to as she entered the café. Her face was striking and somehow unconventional, her nose a perfect wedge. It stuck up over glistening lips and a flat chin that matched the sharp curve of her jaw. Her cheeks were firmer than most. They sat high, and their roundness suggested amusement. Her make-up was visible in the direct sunlight, done with attention to detail, neither underhand nor showy. Diamond bracelets and gold bangles glinted on her wrist. She dropped her suitcase beside the table and sat down opposite me.

'You're buying me a drink,' she said in English.

I had trouble hiding my surprise.

'I am?'

'You are, yes. We are both in need of one.'

The other patrons of the café were staring at us, but she ignored them. I beckoned the waiter over.

'I'm having a coffee,' I said to her. 'What would you like?'

'A real drink.'

'Very well,' I said to the waiter, stammering my way through the French. 'And a beer, too, for me.'

She asked for a Campari and soda, fixing me with a probing stare. I pretended to use a paper napkin to wipe my hands, when in fact I was pulling it apart beneath the table. I tried not to look into her eyes, which were dark hazel and hard as crystal.

'What is your name?' she asked.

'Lawrence. Lawrence Williams. Or Larry, whichever you prefer.'

'You are a Lawrence.'

'If you say so.'

'I do say so. Mine is Élodie Lavelle. One cannot do much with that.'

'No, I guess you can't.'

The drinks arrived. I ignored the coffee and gulped the beer. She did not appreciate this and approached her drink more carefully. I had grown fond of a cold beer while in Madrid, where it was cheaper than water and came with a plate of *chopitos*. Like I had no choice but to get drunk on a warm afternoon.

'Come, you look terrible,' she said, after staring at me in silent fascination. 'What is the matter?'

'I didn't have a ticket booked to Paris. They assured me in Madrid that I could get one at the border.'

'Ah yes. That old story. And when you arrived here they told you that there was a strike.'

'No, they said all the trains to Paris were full.'

'Have you not read the papers?'

'I don't pay much attention to the news.'

'It's this damned pension debacle. The unions are siding with the protestors, so only two trains are leaving tomorrow. Sunday will be the same. I hear that they're protesting up in Paris as we speak.'

This made me wonder if Ethan, my musician flat-mate in Paris, had joined them. He found that sort of thing thrilling, even though the French protests were more like carnivals, complete with singing and dancing.

'So you're stuck here, too?' I said.

'Until tomorrow. The sweet little man has put me on the morning train, the last seat. Perhaps you will have a harder time of it, though?'

'Perhaps.'

We lapsed into silence again. I tried to work out what her beauty might hide. My own appearance hid nothing. My shirt was old and frayed. Her dress could have been bought brand new from the most fashionable of all stores in Paris. But on closer inspection I could see that there was a cigarette burn below the waist.

She leant forward to cover it up.

'Are we going to leave it at that?' she asked.

'Sorry. Of course we aren't. What brings you to this town?'

'That is more like it. I came down here to visit my mother—she is not well. I have no idea why she had to choose the village of Ascain for her retirement. It would not surprise me if she did it to make me travel.'

'Is your mother French?'

'She is, although she claims to be Basque. And yes, my father was English, in case you could not tell. Handy citizenship, although I don't identify with either of them.'

There was something in her accent that was neither French nor English. It reminded me of the transatlantic voices the great American actresses used to put on, in the days when drawling was not permitted on-screen.

She sat up straight as though she had said too much.

'Now Lawrence, you cannot get away that easily. Where are you from?'

'I have no idea where I'm from.'

'Oh. None at all? Why don't we start with where you were born, then?'

'New Zealand. That doesn't exactly help.'

'No wonder your accent is so confused. What draws a small-town boy like you to Paris?'

'I'm about to start my year at the Sorbonne, studying art history.'

This made her wince, as though I had told a lame joke. She raised her thin eyebrows. Every single hair aligned.

'Oh dear. Why would you want to do that? Do you want to be a painter?'

'If I had the talent. Or if I could find the inspiration.'

'Well Lawrence, I cannot think of anything duller than studying something you don't ever want to do.'

'I can't think of anything better. I know, it won't get me anywhere, but it is interesting. Not dull at all.'

'So you were in Madrid. You must have been soaking up that crock of bore in the Prado. You went nowhere near the Thyssen, and you walked through the Reina Sofía but hated everything about it. Too modern and edgy for your liking.'

There was truth to this assessment, even though I did not care to admit it. She had penetrated me. I tried to think of a way to force her back out.

'How did you do that?' I asked. She laughed, and I wondered what there was to laugh about.

'I am enjoying this. You're an open book.'

'Or it was a good guess.' I furrowed my brow. 'So what area would you say I specialise in?'

'You have chosen Paris as your place of study, so my guess is that you specialise in post-Revolutionary Romantic works. And you have positioned yourself close enough to the Louvre so that you can go there every day.'

'Nice try. In fact it's the Impressionists, focussing particularly on the transition from Realism heralded by Manet.'

She drew in her lips. They were attractive lips, but they were also chapped. No amount of lipstick could hide that. She took a cigarette from her handbag and asked if I minded, although I could tell that she would have smoked anyway.

'Do you live in Paris?' I asked.

'I do. A pied-à-terre in the Eighth, one in London, one in New York. I have feet all over the world.'

'Three houses? What do you use them for?'

'Parties, usually. I need a space to entertain.'

'How do you own them? Did you inherit them from your family?'

'My husband owns the ones in Paris and New York. But yes, I did inherit the flat in London.'

She sounded flustered, as though it was too much information to keep track of. I tried not to let my disappointment show at the mention of her husband. There was the danger of treading on somebody's toes. But the danger was also attractive. I started to imagine that I could get to know her, that we could spend the night together. It was a joke to myself, but I imagined feeling her thighs beneath my hands, the thrill of reaching beneath a married woman's dress. It was a ridiculous prospect. I knew nothing about women, except for what I had pieced together from overheard whisperings at school, and the occasional nude painting I had studied. Élodie was like nobody I had ever seen before, and yet she was the epitome of what men were supposed to want. Why had I never come across somebody like her before? And why had women never shown interest in me, until now?

I had no idea what to make of her. She was sitting across the table from me, and I could see those thighs as she crossed them. They were tangible.

'What are you doing tonight?' I asked.

'I thought you would never ask. Who knows what might happen? Needless to say, I am not returning to Ascain.'

'Do you know any hotels in this town?'

'No, sadly. I have never been stuck here before.' She bent in, conspiratorially. 'We should go on an adventure. Biarritz is always nice at this time of the year. Or we could go over the border to San Sebastián.'

'Right. There's one problem, though. I don't have any money.'

'Excuse me?'

'I'm nearly out of cash.'

'How were you planning to pay for a ticket?'

'I don't make many plans.'

'Obviously not.'

'But I have a discount pass, so it shouldn't cost much.'

'That does help.' She disapproved. The concept of a discount must have been foreign to her. 'So you cannot pay for a hotel, or a taxi, or anything. What were you going to do with yourself?'

'I don't know. If worst comes to worst, I thought I could sleep in the train station.'

She laughed, a high flutter that suited her superficial smile.

'Why that's absurd, Lawrence. Luckily for you, I have a soft spot for hopeless causes. Come, we must have some fun while we still can.'

I went to pay for the drinks with the last of my cash. But, before I could, she had laid a platinum credit card on the table. It carried somebody else's name.

'Keep the money,' she said. 'Who knows when you might need it?'

2

There were no taxis outside the train station, so we sat and waited on concrete blocks that were either benches or partitions. Élodie treated hers as a luxurious sofa. She kicked her heels up and busied herself reapplying her make-up. A breeze had come in from the bay, and I took a nondescript black sports jacket from my luggage. She eyed it as if it were a *clochard*'s blanket.

'What's wrong with it?' I asked.

'It is far too big for you. A young man with such an enviable frame as yours needs a good tailor. If we ever make it to Paris, I will show you where to find the very best. And they will teach you not to wear it with an ill-fitted old shirt. It isn't the done thing.'

I took the jacket off again. Inside the station, the Dax train was about to leave. It would not be worth taking, I decided, even if it got me to Paris any faster.

'Where are we going?' I asked.

'In what sense?'

'In all senses.'

'We are going to Biarritz, where there are nice hotels and nice restaurants, neither of which exists around here. Is there a problem with that?'

'What about the hotels around here?'

I was already growing tired of Élodie's insistent snobbery. If she wanted me to feel inferior, then her motive was useless; she had already won on that score. She gave a theatrical shrug, as though she had prepared for this question a long time ago.

'Very well,' she said. 'You stay at the hotel up there.' She gestured to a building across the street with peeling plaster and an ancient drainpipe. 'I will amuse myself.'

'I would if I had any money. Is it really necessary to go all the way to Biarritz for the sake of a hotel?'

'I cannot sleep in an inadequate bed, and nor should you. We must do the best with what we have.'

'And what do we have? Your husband's credit card?'

These words made her quiet. I thought of the joke that I had made to myself, and how wrong it was. She was a married woman, and the rules were different. I began to walk off without much purpose or direction.

'Where are you going?' she called out.

'Wherever I don't have to incur debt to strangers.'

'You won't get far with no money.'

I stopped. She was still sitting on the concrete bench, the picture of composure.

'Don't presume that you know everything about me and my husband, just because of your slight powers of observation.'

'I don't want to know about either of you.'

'We both know what a lie that is. Come back here.'

I disobeyed the order and set off again. The weather was changing—it would be a cool night. I didn't wish to sleep in the drafty station, but I didn't want to entangle myself in whatever game Élodie Lavelle had planned for us either. The addition of a husband made it all the more repulsive. I was above that sort of cruelty.

I had no idea where I was going. The road stretched towards the town centre alongside the station. As it climbed, I could see the Dax train beginning its journey. The overhead lines made a layered backdrop to the scene. The rail yard was rust-coloured, and this matched the barren hill protruding from the Spanish side of the bay. It would have been a Gauguin landscape, if not for the parking lot that stood beside the rail lines. Gnarled trees and low hedges had been planted to divide the lot from the road and they were patchy and untended.

The road steered away from the rail yard and I was confronted by menacing silence. A lone car drove past, the only sound apart from the fading steel wheels on steel track.

I stopped walking, breathing heavily. I needed water. The shops were closed and hostile; their shiny white surfaces reflecting the low sun repelled everything.

It did not take me long to change my mind. She was, after all, my ticket out of Hendaye. She was alluring, and she was interested in me. It felt as though I had already met her a long time ago. Somehow she knew who I was.

I turned to face my reflection in a darkened shop window. My hair was long and curly and tousled from travel, falling over the edge of my collar. The old shirt showed my skinny, pale arms and the faint patch of hair at the top of my chest. I thought of seeing a tailor with Élodie, of wearing a suit that fit me to within an inch and accentuated my slender shape. Her vague promise had released this fantasy in me.

Then I looked closer. The sleepless nights in Madrid had drawn dark circles beneath my eyes, and they would not open wide in the sunlight. I told the uncertain young man staring back that I would not involve myself with this woman any further than I wanted to. But what did I want? There, I told my reflection, was the answer. I smiled at him, and he smiled too, and I set off back in the direction I had come from.

She was waiting for me on the same concrete bench, and she had spread out a newspaper to read. Her eyes did not lift as I drew near. The paper was a few days old.

'Good Lord, that was fast,' she said. 'I was sure it would be for a good half hour before you saw sense.'

I sat down beside her. She folded the paper.

'You get the prize,' I said. 'Did any taxis come in my absence?'

'Not a one.'

'Do you think they might be on strike, too?'

'Who knows?' She tucked the paper into her suitcase. 'Come on, let's go for a walk. You must be in need of some food.'

'Where should we go?'

'Sadly we are not in a gastronomy capital. As I said, I have not been stuck here before. There might be something over by the fishing port.'

I followed her down the same road away from the station. It was admirable how she managed to handle herself in such a tall pair of heels. I scanned the collection of tags and stickers on the suitcase. I could recognise the airport code for Nassau, and a bold United States sticker. Rio de Janeiro, Buenos Aires, Santiago de Chile were there too.

'You've been to South America,' I called to her. She was a few paces ahead. I couldn't keep up with her.

'Well observed, Lawrence.'

The sun had now reached its zenith, and it came out from behind a cloud to beat down on us.

'I do wish I had a hat,' she said. 'Women cannot wear hats these days. I find it very sad.'

'Why can't you wear hats?'

'I have no idea.' She said this wistfully, lost in the distance. I wanted to ask what she was talking about. 'Incidentally, I have nothing to say about South America. I know what you were trying to do there.'

'I was only curious.'

'It was a long time ago. I don't want to think about it.'

The same road was far less intimidating. It crossed over the railway, where the town grew darker. The street was narrow and passed between buildings that were packed tight together. Nobody else was around. The Basque country was alien—clean, with buildings all blindingly white. A strange perversion of heaven. But it was also a timeless place, with no sense of age to it. I couldn't place it in history.

'I do hate it here,' she said, as though reading my mind. 'What a place to be stuck in.'

'I agree. At least the company isn't so bad.'

'Don't say anything like that again, Lawrence, or I will leave you to sleep in the train station. Sentimentality is not welcome, so leave it on the doorstep now.'

'Sorry.'

She began to walk even faster.

'My point, before you interrupted me with that non-sense,' she said, 'was that I don't want to eat a thing in this town. You suit yourself.'

I had eaten nothing since a light breakfast in Madrid, so it was hard to share her nonchalance. I suggested the first café that came into view. It was barely an improvement on the Casa Miguel, but it was more attractive than walking for another half hour. We were in the darkest part of the town now, and the entrance to the café was set back so far and so heavily canopied that it could have been some shady Mafia den. It was easy to imagine a group of old men conspiring in hushed tones at a corner table, but we were the only customers. I ordered a bouillabaisse since fish was the only thing on the menu.

'This is absolutely vile,' Élodie said. I could hardly argue with her. Cigarette ends and spilt drinks littered the floor, though the lighting was dim enough to disguise most of it. 'Your French needs work, by the way. You need to stop saying *please* to everything. It makes you sound even younger than you appear to be.'

'I'm learning,' I said, trying to hide my blush. 'The nuances are always the hardest.'

'Perhaps. And yet you are going to attend lectures that are, I presume, given in French?'

'Yes. I'm worried about it.'

'I can imagine.'

I did my best to eat the bouillabaisse slowly, but animal desire got the better of me.

'Now that cannot be healthy,' she said. 'First you starve yourself, then you inhale a bowl of soup. You will make yourself ill.'

'At least I won't be hungry.'

She grimaced, as though I were an embarrassing child determined to ruin her lunch. I cracked a slice of baguette in half and used this to mop the bottom of the bowl.

'You are so provincial,' she said. 'I hate to think where you learned to eat like that.'

'I'm a peasant at heart,' I said, wiping my mouth with the napkin. 'We all are, really. Are you going to eat anything?'

'I am saving myself for Biarritz. We will have caviar and champagne.'

'Gosh. That's a bit excessive, isn't it?'

'Not at all. It is staple food. I get the feeling that you are not used to this whole business. Let me guess: you flew to Europe economy, always travel discounted. Did you go to Madrid on the couchette? Yes? I thought so. You shared a cabin with five others, all of them disgusting student travellers. You do not stay in hostels, you are too good for that, but I would say that you are most accustomed to a flea-ridden budget hotel on the first ring road, where the breakfast is complimentary but no sane person would want to eat it. Am I correct on that score?'

I had no reply to this, which she took as validation.

'Thank you for reducing me to an ugly stereotype,' I said.

'My pleasure. In any case, you need to be shown an alternative to these boorish ways. Everybody must live the high life at some point. Even students. Now is your time.'

'You're enjoying this, aren't you?'

She showed her teeth for the first time. I had expected them to be as soft as her lips, but instead they were sharp, an uncomfortable detail in her otherwise flawless face. They should have been dangerous, but instead they were curiously inviting.

'What were you doing in Madrid?' she asked. 'Isn't Barcelona a more logical destination at this time of the year?'

'Maybe. I have always wanted to go to Barcelona to see Gaudí. And Miró. Have you ever been there?'

'Of course. But I went there for a party, not to be a tourist. Which is why I have never been to Madrid. Nothing much happens in Madrid. So why would you go there?'

I had no desire to answer the question, simple though it was.

'I went there to see my girlfriend.'

Her eyes widened in a knowing sort of way.

'Ah. Now it all makes sense.'

'No, it doesn't *all make sense*. You don't know me, you don't know her.'

'I do know you. I know you better than anybody else right now. Tell me about her. Who is she? What is her name?'

She took out the cigarettes again, and I was disgusted as she lit up and allowed a haze of smoke to settle over us.

'Sophie. We met in New Zealand. I came over here a few weeks ago to do my studies, and she is studying in New Zealand. But we thought that we could keep seeing each other because her father works in Berlin and she comes over to visit him at least once a year. She didn't want to come to Paris.'

'Why not?'

'She doesn't like it there. So we decided to meet in Madrid for a holiday. Not the most romantic thing I could imagine.' I ran a hand through my hair, as I always did under these circumstances. 'So now she's in Germany with her family. I wasn't invited.'

'Of course you weren't. You are too interesting for them.'

'Excuse me?'

'Oh please, Lawrence. She sounds dull, her family sounds dull. I know the type.' She drew on her cigarette. 'You are in love with her, aren't you?'

'I don't know what I am.'

'Is she in love with you?'

'Maybe. I couldn't say.'

'She *is* in love with you. I knew it. How obvious. You are just the type, of course. Stiff and awkward, pretending to be cultured, pretending not to care about her feelings but then unexpectedly giving her a dollop of sentimentality. How old is she?'

'Twenty. Same as me.'

'Is this your first relationship?'

'First serious one.'

'What about for her?' I became quiet. Élodie could not contain her delight. 'Oh dear. You poor young man. I hope that you aren't intent on breaking her precious little heart.'

'Why do I get the feeling that you're an expert on heartbreak?'

She smiled indulgently, conceding a small defeat. 'You really oughtn't,' she said. 'Besides, we're not talking about me. I would suggest cutting romance out of the equation while you're young. She might never learn, but at least you will. And don't let it get too complicated. That way lies disaster. What was she like in Madrid?'

'It was fine. She enjoys art, too, so that helped. We talked a lot about Goya. She's the sort of person who can stand in front of *La Maja Vestida* and tell you everything there is to know about it. I think she sees paintings the way I see them.'

'And did you make *love* to her?'

She drew the phrase out as though the whole thing were a joke. I tried unsuccessfully to keep my expression blank. She grinned.

'I know that look, Lawrence. I am sure you make a divine couple. Are you both virgins?'

'It's none of your business.'

'I knew it. And how long have you been seeing her?'

I hoped that I could get away without answering. But she sat forward and waited. The truth of the matter was that we had not made love in Madrid, and I was not sure why. Everything had been congenial, but nothing had happened. And so I had left disappointed with myself. Why did I not know what to do in those situations? Why did everything have to be so formal and forced around Sophie?

'For a few months before I left New Zealand,' I replied.

'My word,' Élodie said, her amusement plain. 'We have work to do, my friend. I have no idea whom I should feel the more sorry for: you or her. It is a perfect balance. My advice is to end it as soon as you can.'

'Hey, I never asked for your advice. I do like her. A lot. You're making an awful lot of presumptions.'

'Maybe I am. It is rather funny, though. When do you plan on seeing her next?'

'I don't know. She might come over here in December.'

'At least you are keeping it indefinite. And now we must go for a walk. I need to know every last sordid detail.'

I might have been furious with her, but she paid for my bouillabaisse, which I could feel sitting on my stomach. The locals stared as we left, as though we were an exotic species. Élodie was, and her genus was a rare one. But it was also one that could bite.

3

The town was deserted. I asked Élodie where we should go, and she stopped on the corner and cast around for an answer.

'We can go to the old docks,' she said. 'And we shall see where that takes us.'

Having no better suggestion, I followed her down a steep street. The houses here were more dilapidated, slipping towards the water. I imagined that the merest tremor would send them crashing over one another into the bay. A power cable hung loose from one of the villas and it now swayed in the breeze. This part of the town was stuck somewhere between the rusty grime of the rail yards and the sleepy old fishing port, which was all barnacles and salt. Both were untended and ugly, and yet something about this scene pleased me. I did not wish to disturb it.

'You are so quiet, boy,' she said. I had been listening

to the sound of her heels on the cobblestones. 'What is the matter with you?'

'Nothing,' I said without conviction. Her eyes were hidden behind the sunglasses, but I imagined they were boring into me.

'Now really, Lawrence, I cannot support this. Is it because I mocked you and your little princess?'

'No. Yes. I imagine you're used to people reacting strongly to your insults.'

'I'm not, as a matter of fact. You are the first one to take things so personally.'

'You can't get much more personal.'

She swayed her head dreamily. The street widened to a square, which was paved with red stone and over-looked the port. It was lined with old stone balustrades, which were also crumbling. The lampposts had sirens attached to them. I knew this was common in French towns—sometimes you heard them in Paris—and yet there was something sinister about them here. It felt as though we were treading on enemy territory. Élodie was more concerned by her appearance than her surroundings. She would draw a hand up to her hair every minute or so and rearrange some part of it.

'We can admire the view from here,' Élodie said. She led me onto the terrace and leant against the balustrades. 'For what it is. I don't like this atmosphere.'

The afternoon sun had dipped and lit the bay, while the town behind us was bathed in shadow from the surrounding hills. The fishing boats and pleasure yachts stood side-by-side, all shining in the sunlight. Morisot could have painted this harbour, but it would never have been so crystalline. I would gladly have stood there for the rest of the day.

'It's not so bad, is it?' I said, gesturing to the bay. 'Why do we need to go to Biarritz when we have this?'

'Trust me. Biarritz will have you eating your words. There is nothing spectacular about any of this.'

'You would prefer a spectacle?'

'Of course. I would rather be impressed than under-whelmed.'

I would have said the same before first going to Paris a few weeks earlier. It surprised me that anybody with Élodie's apparent wisdom and experience might hold this shallow view.

'I hope you prove me wrong,' I said. I had to stoop to lean on the balustrade; it was designed for a person of her height.

'This simply will not do,' she said. 'You must tell me more about the girl. She is smarter than most, I presume.'

'What makes you think that?'

'You met her at university. And you would never even consider a relationship with an uneducated girl. Your parents would not allow it, in the first place.'

'You think you know everything,' I said. Had she already made up her mind about me?

'That's because I do. And is she timid? Or does she mask all of her insecurities with a brave public face?'

'You're not describing yourself there, are you?'

'Oh how funny, Lawrence. Maybe you really are more perceptive than I gave you credit for. But tell me about her, or I will have to tell you.'

I tried to think of something that I could say about Sophie. What could I tell Élodie? She had long straw hair and a few freckles across her nose, and when we talked about art we could have been sharing some great secret, something that set us apart from everybody else. But it felt as though I could never really know her, even if she knew me.

I was distracted as a man walked past us with a child on his shoulders. They bobbed up and down the steep street. He walked with purpose and talked in Basque to the little boy. The tongue was alien to me, but it sounded gentle and kind.

'All right,' I said, once they had walked out of sight. 'She's a nice person, and I like her for that reason.'

'Oh dear. It really is worse than I feared.'

She started to walk down a narrow street that wound its way towards the waterfront. There was an impressive statue, which I did not recognise, on one of the corners. It was a Madonna and Child, and the interaction between the two figures was more intimate than usual. The Madonna held something in her free hand that might have been an apple, but I could neither recognise it nor understand its significance. The walls around this part of the street were made from an earthy sort of stone, which I liked better than the clean whitewashing everywhere else.

'So you like her because she is nice,' Élodie continued, as though she had been giving the matter careful thought. 'And what do you want to do? Do you want to marry her?'

'Of course not,' I said, with more feeling than I had intended. 'People don't get married young these days.'

Élodie's expression was sympathetic, but she did not say anything.

We walked along the waterfront, where the road was lined with upturned fishing boats. They were all colourful, a relief from the uniform white.

Seeing the ocean so close made me yearn for a swim, if only to wash away the musty smell that had been clinging to me since Madrid and my last shower. I thought about how it would be to swim with Élodie. I could see her figure cutting through the water, her legs moving in tandem and her arms spreading out gracefully. In my imagination her body became one with the water. I would paddle and splash, but she would swim as though she were dancing.

We reached the end of the street. The boats were

swaying on the bay. Élodie was smirking for some reason. It began to irritate me.

'What is it?'

'Nothing,' she replied. 'You just happen to be very amusing. Come, let's leave this horrid town. There must be a taxi by now.'

The walk back to the station did not feel as long. And there were two taxis waiting. One was a Renault, the other a Mercedes. Élodie chose the Mercedes.

'I have to ask,' she said, once we were next to each other in the taxi. 'Why did you choose to take the train? Was there no despicable low-cost flight from Madrid to Paris?'

'I prefer to take the train. There is something grand about it. And I like being able to see the land.'

The road wound around a bluff and out of the town, following the seaside. The landscape remained beautiful —green and stately, but also wild—and the ochre rocks on the coastline were arranged in strata. I preferred this untended nature to the Parisian sculptural aesthetic. The parks there were designed pedantically along lines of symmetry, asserting dominance over growth. They made the city more stunted and static than it already was.

'Is she pretty?' Élodie asked. She must have been staring at me for all of this time.

'Who?'

'Your girlfriend, or whatever she is.'

'Why are you so obsessed with her?'

'Why are you so protective of her? Surely there is nothing to be ashamed of.'

'There isn't. Pretty is the wrong word, though.'

'Why? Do you think I'm pretty?'

I took Élodie in, from her pointed toe to her almost masculine jaw.

'No,' I said. 'Pretty is the wrong word for you.'

'Good. I ask because I cannot imagine her being pre-occupied with her appearance.'

'Aren't most women?'

'Christ. Clearly you haven't met many of them. But she is not a radiant beauty, is she?'

'That depends on the definition. You want me to tell you how radiantly beautiful you are, don't you?'

'I don't need to be told that, least of all from a nervous young art history student.'

'You wouldn't find it reassuring?'

'Not in the slightest. Quite the opposite, in fact. And the girl has to be pretty. Otherwise you would not be wasting your time.'

I wished she would stop talking about Sophie. It felt wrong to be talking about her to a stranger—let alone one who criticised her so openly.

'In that case,' I said, 'why do you want to know about her? You're not jealous, are you?'

She cast a look of dead seriousness at me. It was and still is a horrific stencil on my mind. The car became quiet. I could feel the blush creeping up my cheeks again and begged it to go away.

'I am afraid to ask,' she said. 'But have you any other clothes?'

'Not many.'

'I can see them already. We must find you something in Biarritz, or they will not let us in the hotel.'

'Like what?'

The distance between us had grown. She curled her body up against the door, and when she turned to survey me it was with reproof. She opened her mouth, showing those sharp teeth, and spent a while judging me in silence.

'The jacket will do,' she said. 'Where did you get it?'

'In Paris, at the Galeries Lafayette.' I said this with a shade of pride, even though I knew that she would not approve. I might as well have told a joke at my own expense.

'On sale, no doubt. But it will do. The rest needs work.'

'The rest?'

'Yes, the rest.' My suitcase was small. I had packed three changes of clothes, and I had not provided for this disruption, so I was awash with stale sweat. The shirt was accompanied by an old pair of jeans and shoes that were falling apart. Perhaps she had a point.

'So what do you suggest?'

'I hardly need to think about it, in your case. White shirt with a subtle pattern, and cufflinks that are neither too showy nor too silly. Too many men wear bad cufflinks. And a thin black tie. Do you have a pair of sunglasses? In fact, no, I don't want to know. We will buy a pair.'

I had never worn cufflinks before, and my striped school tie was the only one that I had ever owned.

'How charitable of you,' I said.

'It is for a good cause. And it is not my charity, remember.'

'Won't your husband wonder about all these purchases on his credit card?'

She returned her sunglasses to her nose. 'Not to worry. I always have a story for these things.'

The road passed through Saint-Jean-de-Luz, with its postcard-worthy fishing port and little else. This part of the world was once the place to be. The Modernists and the Romantics all described it in detail: the perfect climate and beaches, the rugged beauty of the landscape. It was hard to deny that all of this existed now, but it was preserved and distorted. I thought that whatever spirit I had seen in paintings and read about in books was no longer there.

'I am happy to have met you, Lawrence,' Élodie said as the taxi passed the town limits, where the traffic was thinning. 'You are so much more interesting than the bores that I am usually exposed to. And you are handsome, too, under the bad haircut.'

I had never thought of myself in this way before.

'Not in a normal way,' she continued with surprising earnestness. 'But then, nor would I want you to be. You do need work, though. We can fix you yet.'

'For a moment there I thought you might have been complimenting me.'

'No, it was a compliment. You have potential. Most people do not.'

4

She kept silent as we drove north along the bay. Soon huts and villas on the seaside were replaced by terraced apartment blocks. The increase in wealth, if not taste, was conspicuous. The cafés had big wicker chairs and opened onto a terrace. There were galleries and clothes shops and pâtisseries with window displays and warm golden lights.

Élodie waited until we were on the main shopping street before instructing the driver to pull over. He left the meter running.

'This is just the place,' she said. The pavement was cobbled and lined with a heavy set of trees, all of which were manicured.

'It's a playground for the rich, isn't it?'

'I have always liked playgrounds. They are a lot of fun.'

The street could have been a miniature of the Rue de Rivoli, but without any *clochards* or cigarette ends clogging the gutters. The café terraces and charcuteries were all there, as were any number of international chain stores with their familiar labels. Élodie bypassed them. Her destination was more discreet, hidden away in an arcade. I imagined that nobody but frequent visitors to Biarritz would know of it.

She could not find exactly what she wanted, but as I faced myself in the mirror, I saw somebody else. There was something exhilarating about it, though it was frightening too. The tie was a match to her specifications—long, thin and black—while the shirt was a light shade of blue. In the end she did buy a navy blue jacket and white trousers as well, and a pair of reflective sunglasses with a light frame. She said that this jet-set look suited me better—that I could have stepped out of a Fellini film. I tried to believe her. The white trousers were a revelation. I had never owned such an outfit before.

Ethan would be beside himself with envy or mockery. I thought about him as Élodie leant against the counter to sign her receipt, running her high-heeled shoe up and down her calf. Ethan knew about women. He went out for drinks with them, painting himself as a bohemian wanderer who sought nothing but pleasure. They loved him for it. They shared a bottle of wine and listened, captivated, while he told his stories. Every weekend there was somebody else in his bed. He would tell me of his exploits the next day, and I would feign disapproval when in fact I envied his audacity.

We had met at school, where we were both oddities for different reasons. Ethan revelled in his own strangeness, while I was too shy to acknowledge mine. But he was genuine. He meant everything he said.

Since we had started living together, he had taken delight in teasing me, labelling me as the aesthete who read books and visited art galleries all day and went to bed with a cup of tea. But I could take it from him, because it was affectionate, and in turn I could tell him what a *poseur* he was. It never offended him. On the contrary, he took it as a compliment. He might have been a philanderer, but he had never met a woman like Élodie. How often did anybody meet a woman like Élodie?

We returned to the taxi a half hour later and drove to the seaside promenade, passing the casino and the first string of hotels. The beachfront was a simple golden slice out of the coastline. It reminded me of an Impressionist painting I had studied, where everything was just the right colour and people walked along the sand in suits and ties. That was a distant time, when society was inscribed with too many rules and conventions to keep track of.

Now I could not see a single figure on the beach with a shirt on. And there I was in a jacket and tie and white trousers, reinforcing those conventions. The late-season revellers were out in force. They swarmed into the ocean in the shape of a Japanese fan, overwhelming the beach. Élodie was looking out the window, too, but I could tell that she was not thinking the same thoughts.

'Thank you,' I said. 'I don't know if I can repay you for this.'

'You have to stop thanking me, Lawrence. It does not suit you in those clothes.'

This was true. I pulled the new sunglasses down to block out the late-afternoon beam hanging over the water.

The hotel was through a set of gates at the end of the promenade, set in the middle of lawns and topiaries. It was awe-inspiring. The Second Empire decadence of the architecture gave it a Napoleonic stiffness that was out of place with its natural surroundings. It was a microcosm of Paris, complete with a mansard roof and flourishes of decorative detail. I tried to guess what lay behind the pastel red walls and the drawn blinds. It was sure to be an improvement on the floor of the Gare d'Hendaye.

'Well, I can't say that I'm surprised,' I said as the taxi deposited us at the entrance. A white-gloved man in uniform took our luggage. 'You would choose this sort of a hotel, wouldn't you?'

'This is the Palais, darling. We must live as well as we can.'

I stood marvelling at it all while Élodie paid the driver

and the porters took our luggage in a golden cart. My eyes moved from the luxury sedans and sports vehicles to the window boxes and potted plants, which were meticulously trimmed. All of the colours were accentuated, as though they had been digitally enhanced for a postcard. Everything that was not reflective was reflected in something else.

'What's it to be?' Élodie asked as we entered through the revolving door. I was straggling behind her open-armed swagger. 'A Royal Suite, or an Imperial Suite? It's either Churchill or Wallis Simpson.'

'A suite? Isn't that a bit much for one night?'

'More than a bit. We could do a Prestige Room, but it will have to overlook the sea. I can't stand a view into the courtyard.' She thought about this. 'No, it must be a suite. Come.'

The lobby was a sibling to the courtyard. I tried to walk lightly on the marble tiles, in case I slid on their burnished surface and knocked over a vase or a bust. The tiles, too, reflected a mirror-world. I couldn't tell which was more real—the chandeliers or their blurred counterparts in the floor.

I followed Élodie to the reception desk, where the clerk informed her that there were no free rooms.

'Royal Suite it is,' she said to me. 'Such a shame. I did always prefer Mrs Simpson's taste.' She turned to the clerk and ordered Veuve Clicquot and Aquitaine caviar to be brought up directly. I wanted to grab her by the arm as she handed over her husband's credit card, but I restrained myself.

This was it, I thought: one night, and then I would never have to worry about her again. I could embellish the details when I told Ethan. For once I would be the one with a real exploit to recount.

'This is excessive,' I said as we walked up the winding staircase.

'Isn't it, though? Don't worry. I am not doing it for your sake.'

'You've been here before, haven't you?'

'Of course I have, you silly boy. I've been everywhere. And this is one of the few remaining enclaves of true magic. You will learn to love it, trust me.'

The details—there were so many of them—leapt out at random. Everything was gilded and chintzy. Paintings, cabinets, mirrors, statues and flowers occupied every spare space. I tried to remind myself that all of this was the habitat of distorted romanticism, even if it was also *true magic*. But what was *true magic*? It sounded like a contradiction. Was this the sort of place where the truth and illusion intersected? The luxury that surrounded me was real, but it was also fake.

The suite was appropriately palatial. I went through its features as though they were part of a grand checklist:

the ocean view, the velvety curtains, the flowers threatening to consume each and every surface, and the paintings cluttering the walls.

Out on the terrace the champagne and caviar were waiting for us on a silver tray, the ice bucket perspiring in the heat. I should have taken the initiative and poured into the two awaiting glasses, but Élodie was already striding out there, shedding her travelling jacket and allowing it to drop onto the sun-drenched tiles. I followed her and took a glass, telling myself to stop staring at her shoulders. She flexed them and their curves were accentuated. Her dress hung off them as though it were an extension of her body.

'What should we drink to?' I asked, pretending that the line had come to me from a film script. I tried not to let my nerves show, but they slipped through somehow.

'Don't be silly, Lawrence. Let the drink be what it is. The celebration can come later.'

I raised my glass anyway, and she bit back her laughter. The champagne was acidic and sweet, but it was refreshing. I could see myself becoming fond of it.

'I must change out of these rags,' Élodie said, swirling the champagne around her mouth and savouring it. 'Please excuse me. You amuse yourself out here.'

I watched her back as she returned to the main room. It was visible above the hemline, and I could see that it was as brown as the rest of her skin. The tan was complemented by a few conspicuous moles. There was what appeared to be a small white scar running down her shoulderblade, and I would not have noticed it had it not stood out so pronounced from the dark skin around it. I tried a tentative bite of the caviar on a blini. It was rough and salty, and I wanted to spit it out. It was hard to imagine why anybody might pay good money for it.

From the railing I had a view out onto the beach, and beyond to the ocean. The horizon line in Europe was different. In New Zealand it was a rigid contrast of dark sea to light sky, the two drawn apart as if with a pencil and a ruler. The ocean was never this blue, or the beaches this golden.

I stood admiring it for a long while. It was remarkable to find myself so elevated. The people on the beach appeared much further away than I knew them to be.

As I went to the tray of caviar my eye was snagged. Élodie had forgotten to pull the bedroom curtains. Usually my reaction would have been to turn away. Instead I caught my breath as she bent over to find something in her suitcase. She really was brown all over. I had failed to notice the ideal shape of her frame from beneath the dress, but naked it made me think of the Aphrodite torsos that I had seen in the Louvre.

I turned away. She must have intended that. She had more sense than to let herself be seen. The thought of confronting her again was becoming too much to bear. And the thought of reaching around those thighs was becoming less of a joke. This made me no better than a voyeur, and I told myself to stop. I left her to continue dressing and leant over the ornamental parapet.

My thoughts turned to Sophie. Would she have enjoyed herself here? Her tastes were simpler than champagne and caviar. But perhaps champagne and caviar were an aspiration for her as much as they were for Élodie, and perhaps she had wanted them when we were in Madrid. I asked her where she wanted to go for dinner, what she wanted to drink, but I never asked what she really wanted.

A waft of understated perfume announced Élodie's return. She wore a shiny purple gown that fell to the knee and was cut deep at the back. She might have read my mind. I held the tray of caviar out for her, my hand shaking.

'How chivalrous you are, Lawrence,' she said in a more sensuous voice than I had heard before. 'You must be learning. Remember what I said, though: Don't tell me how beautiful I look.'

'Don't worry. I wasn't going to. You look pretentious and fake.'

'Ah.' She put the blini to her lips in an impossibly suggestive way. 'You *are* learning. You are being insincere.'

'I wasn't trying to be anything. How you interpret these things is entirely up to you.'

'Come now. You can't win, Lawrence.'

She took the tray of caviar and replaced it on the table. Her body edged closer to mine, and I was pushed backwards towards the balustrades. I felt my panic rising.

'Stop, Élodie, please.'

I ducked away and rounded her. Nobody had ever approached me in this way before. What was I meant to do? It was unsettling, but like an electric shock it was also thrilling. I could have touched her then, and I could have run my hand down her back with the moles and the scar. Her breath could have been an inch from mine. Instead I was paralysed.

'What the hell is wrong with you?' I said.

'I wanted to show you a few more secrets.'

'I'm sure you did. Who are you?'

I was in the middle of the terrace with my arms at my side, suddenly feeling debased in these new clothes that really did belong in a Fellini film.

'I am whoever you want me to be,' Élodie purred.

'Sure. Prostitutes say that. Are you a prostitute? Have you stolen your client's credit card? It wouldn't surprise me.'

She cast her gaze down at the tiles, which were baking beneath the sun, and she scratched her neck. She remained alluring despite her irritation.

'You don't have to give this the theatrical treatment, you silly boy. You are too young to understand.'

'Just tell me who you are. Return the favour at least.'

'What do you want to know? I can tell you anything.'

This was true, I thought. She had plenty of stories in her arsenal. I remained facing her for a while, trying to think of a way to expose her.

'I keep forgetting how young you are,' she said.

'So how old are you?'

She could have been anywhere over thirty. She was a different person from every angle.

'You can ask me that later, when I'm a little more drunk and you're a little less prudish.' She abandoned the champagne. 'Let's go to the bar. I need a drink. A *proper* drink.'

The sun would soon set. I wanted to stay on the terrace to watch it. I could tell that it was about to dip below the last layer of cloud and bathe the scene in gold. But it was clear to me now that Élodie Lavelle was not accustomed to denial. I could not have left her, had I wanted to. Her will was stronger than mine. She extended her arm, and I took it tentatively. I was the last in a line of jewellery pieces adorning her, somewhere below the gold ring on her hand. The band was inscribed, but I could not make out the words.

5

Although it was early in the evening, the bar was full. Light cocktail piano played in the background. It suited the atmosphere. Even in my new jacket and tie I felt underdressed, and I was by far the youngest person in the room. They might have smelt my discomfort. I stood on the shore by a sea of dinner jackets.

'Should we have bought a dinner suit?' I asked, as quietly as I could. 'I'm feeling a little out of place.'

'Nonsense. I want you to stand out.' She leant at the bar. All of the other ladies in the room were seated. 'It is very important to stand out, Lawrence. You might as well be anyone, otherwise. What are you drinking?'

'I don't know.'

'Have a daiquirí.'

'I've never had one before.'

'There is a first time for everything. Not to worry. You

will be drinking Scotch whisky by the end of the evening.'

She said this with such certainty that I could not disagree. She ordered another Campari and soda. I asked her if this was routine.

'When your life is as chaotic as mine, you want some routines,' she said.

She used the straw to stir her drink and studied the bobbing ice cubes.

'May I try it?' I said.

'Certainly not. It is my drink.'

'And what does that mean?'

'Nothing.' She swayed her head so that her hair moved without coming out of its arrangement. 'Where shall we go? Shall we take a table?'

'Why not?'

I followed her in the direction of a free corner table. But before we could reach it, she swept down on one of the fellow patrons, who was himself sitting at a table, and kissed him on the neck.

'Guess who?' she said into his ear.

He was a dark-haired man in his forties. His belt was a notch too tight. I felt a rush.

'Why, Élodie,' he said in a New York accent. 'What in the hell are you doing here of all places?'

'You know me. I always have to be where the party is.'

'Quite right. And who's this?' He gazed at me, in a way

that was irritatingly casual. 'Illegitimate son?' He laughed at his joke, while I stood to the side and wished that he would stop.

Élodie joined in.

'Oh, wouldn't that be funny?' she said. She accentuated the English streak in her accent, leaving any trace of a drawl behind. 'No. I met this lad at the station in Hendaye, if you can believe it.'

'Hendaye? What were you doing there? Wait, sit down, then tell me.'

He was with a woman who had permed hair and wore a shiny gold dress. He gestured for the waiter to bring two more chairs over. I felt sick. I wanted to be on the roof terrace with Élodie again, talking about something real and drinking champagne, not this disgusting cocktail. I was beginning to realise how much I enjoyed talking to her. The man extended a hand, and I took it, feeling a much tighter grip than my own.

'I'm Lawrence,' I said. I had been lingering for too long. My palm was wet, and I felt it slip against his callused skin.

'Ed Selvin. Pleasure to meet you, Larry.'

From across the tabletop I could see that he had the smile of a terrier. I tried to move my chair nearer to Élodie, but she stuck close to Selvin. The other woman was never introduced, although she feigned some interest in our conversation. She wore too much eyeliner, which smothered the life out of her eyes. Like an unoriginal landscape painting, she faded into the background.

'You have a lot of explaining to do, young lady,' Selvin said in a tone that was neither jovial nor serious. 'What's going on here?'

'I've agreed to show my new friend the high life,' she said.

Selvin raised his eyebrows, which were effeminate and thin. 'Well you came to the right place, let me tell you.'

'He has no money, would you believe? And of course, with those damned rail workers on strike, he won't be in Paris for days.'

'Wow, Élodie. I never picked you for the charitable type. Is this some sentimental ageing thing?'

'Now really, darling, that is too cruel. Besides, you wrote the handbook on ageing, didn't you? Midlife crisis over yet?'

'Had it twenty years ago. It's out of my system.'

The conversation was humiliating. I tried the daiquirí. It was both bitter and sweet, and very strong.

'What do you do, Larry?' Selvin asked.

'I'm a student of art history,' I said, much to Élodie's evident displeasure. 'At the Sorbonne.'

'How coincidental. I run an art dealership in New York.'

'Do you?'

It was a joke, and it meant something to Élodie.

'No, not really,' he said. 'Do you consider yourself more of an artist or a connoisseur?'

'Neither.'

'Right. So what are you, then?'

'I'm not sure yet.'

Selvin waited for me to elaborate. And then he laughed, a mocking, self-righteous noise, and I should have got up and walked away. Élodie joined in, in much the same tone, but it did not suit her as it suited him.

'Go easy on the boy, Ed,' she said. 'He's learning.'

'Sure, sure.' Selvin drank deep from his whisky, relishing the bite. He had the beginnings of a beard, which was grey around the edges. He wore his wealth explicitly. His suit was expensive, but it clung too tight around the shoulders and accentuated his meaty gut. His drooping eyelids said that he was drunk. This was how the rich survived their dull lives: by pouring liquor down their throats for half the day.

Fortunately he returned his attention to Élodie. She did not want to give her reasons for being in Hendaye, and I thought it was strange that she did not mention her mother in Ascain. Instead she continued to exchange repartee with Selvin. They got on well, and their jousting played in harmony. It was both enviable and deplorable.

'Are you still with that bozo in Paris?' he asked.

Élodie's eyelids fluttered. It was the only hint of her discomfort.

'What was his name again? Marcel?'

'He doesn't stop me from having fun. Have you seen my beautiful ring?' She laid her hand in the middle of the table. I leant forward to read the inscription, which glinted in the light. *Nous sommes nés magnifiques.* I could translate it, but the phrase meant nothing to me. 'I will sell it for a fortune one day.'

'Of course you will. Hey, why not sell it now? Then you could buy me a drink.'

'I have money, you silly man. It just isn't mine.'

'Ah, the best sort.' It seemed as if he was about to say something to me—his diaphragm drew in and he sat up—but he continued talking to Élodie. 'We need to have a word later,' he said. He did not intend for me to hear.

'I agree,' she said. 'We should. How long are you here for?'

Selvin positioned himself so that I would be unable to hear his reply. I was surprised that he could speak at such a low volume, when he had been so loud and energetic. Despite my curiosity it felt impolite to listen in, so I directed my attention to the nameless woman. She was attractive in a more conventional way than Élodie. Her hair was golden and clashed with her fake tan. She was not European. I could tell how uneasy she was in her lavish surroundings. This French decadence was an alien concept, even newer for her than it was for me. I was about to introduce myself, but I thought that this might be rude. I presumed there was a reason she had not been introduced and I struggled to guess what it could be.

I turned back and watched Élodie. She was animated and enthusiastic with Selvin, but her eyes were hollow. It was impossible to tell whether she was relaxed or uneasy. She leant away from me, making Selvin her sole objective. She drew her feet up off the floor, her shoes gleaming in the light. They must have been uncomfortable, with their high-arched curves and tight fastenings.

A waiter brought over plates of olives and cheeses, for which I was glad. It gave me something to do. I thanked him, while Selvin and Élodie ignored both him and the food. Then Selvin took a call on his mobile phone, and wandered over to a dark corner of the bar, putting a finger to his ear to block out the noise.

'I must say,' Élodie said to me, 'I refuse to be chained to a phone. Fewer intrusions.'

'Yes,' I said. 'Although it might have helped me today.'

Both Ethan and Sophie would be wondering where I had got to. Sophie liked to talk often, even from the other side of the world, and it was liberating to think that we were truly out of contact for the first time. But I pushed this thought away.

'You don't have a mobile phone?' she said. 'Goodness. I thought that everybody your age had one.'

'I must be the exception. I know, it's old-fashioned, but it keeps things simpler.'

'There is nothing wrong with being old-fashioned.'

When Selvin returned he drained the whisky glass of its last amber drop and set it down so heavily that the table shook.

'Vanessa and I need to go find some dinner,' he said, taking his newly named companion by the arm. 'Hope you don't mind. We'll see you later, I'm sure.'

'Not at all,' Élodie said, betraying a certain disappointment. 'It's not a bit early for dinner?'

'No, it isn't.'

Vanessa had not finished her drink. He held her around the middle, which was awkward due to his girth.

I waited until they had cleared the bar before rounding on Élodie.

'Who is *he*?' I asked, thinking that in some ways the answer was less important than the question.

'An old friend,' she said. 'I don't know where he found his wealth. Just one of those fellows who was born poor and decided to make himself rich. He's fun, isn't he?'

'If that's how you define fun. How did you meet?'

'Years ago. He has something to do with film. It was a party in Cannes. We danced on the beach. But that was another lifetime. He's changed, I've changed.'

'You could always dance on the beach with him here. I'm sure he's more your equal.'

I must have sounded more woeful than I had intended, because she became mockingly sympathetic.

'Oh Lawrence. I only want to dance on the beach with you. There, is that better? Those clothes become you, by the way. You are doing well, boy.'

'Please don't call me that.'

'What? *Boy*? I will if you stop acting like one.'

I suddenly wanted to kiss her. I imagined how her mouth would feel. I could taste the oil of her lipstick and smell her perfume on my collar. But this was another joke, I told myself, born of the drink. I held up the daiquirí and took another gulp. Yes, I thought, that was definitely it. I took one of the olives and rolled it around my mouth.

'Why were you at a party in Cannes?' I asked.

Élodie's attention turned to the terrace beyond the windows, and she folded and unfolded her legs. A crease appeared in her thigh, but then it smoothed out again, the lone disruption a mole beneath her knee.

'Are you an actress?' I continued. After all, it had been playing on my mind.

She was pained, but then she pulled her mouth into a defiant line.

'Yes, that's it. I never did anything very popular. I have been out of that game for years.'

She said this with a shade of regret. She had the appearance of an ex-actress. Her beauty was enhanced and preserved with what I presumed to be surgery.

'That makes sense,' I said. 'Why didn't you tell me that before, when I asked who you were?'

'Because it isn't who I am.' Her voice had lost its breezy tone. 'I've moved on. And besides, Ed has his own life.'

'I thought he was interested in you,' I said. 'Or is the feeling mutual?'

'None of that cheek.' She reclined in her chair and ran a hand along the surface of her hair. Her mouth was downturned. She was judging me, and this judgement was more powerful than her expression. 'Lawrence, darling; are you really jealous?'

'Only as jealous as you are of Sophie.'

'But you have every reason to envy Ed. You really should aspire to him. He has lived a full life.'

'I knew it. You are interested in him.'

I could not remember the last time that I had talked to anybody so flirtatiously.

'Silly boy. Leave those clichés alone. They need a master's hand.'

She picked up her purse, which matched the purple of her dress. She held it close to her chest and drew her shoulders in. They were limber, and they must have been strong.

'Come on,' she said. 'I want to run into more people.'

She had finished her drink, while mine was untouched. I forced myself to down it. The flavour had improved. I wondered if this was because the sugar collected in the bottom of the martini glass, or if my palate was seizing up under the burn of the alcohol. As usual, I had no answer for my own question.

'How many people do you know in this place?' I asked.

'Who could say? It is the high season, so anybody could turn up here. When you've travelled as much as I have you will understand how small the world is.'

She sounded a little intoxicated already, which did nothing to improve my image of her. But then, I thought, perhaps it was for show. She dropped those impractical heels to the carpet, and I followed her out towards the terrace, watching for any sign of discomfort. I knew, even then, that this was unlikely. She was the actress, after all.

6

Élodie lit up another cigarette on the terrace. We were by the swimming pool, which afforded a fine view across the ocean and over to the dense line of buildings on the bluff. The beach was emptying, but with a fresh gust of wind I could see that the surfers were out on the rip-tide.

'Are you having fun, Lawrence?' Élodie asked, inhaling deeply so that her voice became huskier.

'Sure I am.'

She tapped the ash from the decaying cigarette to the tiles.

'That really is bad for you, you know,' I said.

'I know. Have you not noticed? I do many things that are bad for me.'

'Why?'

'Because it is who I am.'

She held the cigarette out to me. I put up a hand.

'I've never smoked,' I said. 'And I don't plan on starting now.'

'Really, Lawrence, you must try. One puff won't hurt. Look at me—I've been smoking since I was twelve. Do I appear ill?'

I tried to find some sign of the rotting carcass beneath the make-up and jewellery. She had angled herself as though she were in the middle of a photo shoot.

'No,' I said, failing to hide my reproof. 'You've covered it very carefully. I'm not capable of doing that.'

'One puff and I will let you off.'

Resigned, I took the white stick and pressed it to my lips. It was as if I had inhaled a mixture of burnt tar and ashes. I coughed, but tried to subdue it. Élodie took the smouldering torture device back. It left a crude aftertaste.

'Not to your liking? Don't worry. One does get used to these things. Good thing Ed didn't offer you a cigar.'

'Are they stronger than this?'

'They are utterly divine. There is nothing like a good cigar. It is the difference between a *cafetière* and a strong espresso. Incomparable.' She took another puff of the cigarette and grimaced. 'I only have these out of necessity. If it were possible I would be smoking five Montecristos a day. Even my husband's credit wouldn't extend that far. But do give smoking a chance. It gets better. One cannot say that about many things.'

———

'But it really is unhealthy.'

'Isn't everything? Coffee, alcohol, that bouillabaisse. They all do harmful things to the body, but we enjoy them.'

The sun was on its path towards the horizon. It would take another hour or two to set, but the terrace was already bathed in the deep gold of a day's end. It shimmered on the water, and it all felt wrong. Unlike Hendaye, with its hostile townspeople and a blaring white sun, this terrace felt like a Hollywood film set.

'Where do you live in Paris, Lawrence?' she asked, as she continued to lean on the parapet, her shoulderblades pointing out to sea.

'The Sixth,' I said as casually as I could. It was a fashionable address that suggested more money than I had. 'I have a little one-bedroom. Rue Saint-Sulpice.'

'Good Lord. I had you down as the Thirteenth at best. What possessed you to live there? How do you afford it?'

'An aunt left me some money. And my flatmate is meant to be contributing.'

'He is not French, is he? Or she?'

'Ethan is from New Zealand. He's a musician, and he is doing well for himself. But he is younger than me, and he doesn't know how to share a house.'

'Fancy that. Two clueless boys living in Rue Saint-Sulpice. Let me guess—your parents must have had a hand in this arrangement.'

'I came here to get away from them. And I thought that this would be the best way to spend my money. Enjoying life while it lasts, right?'

'Good for you, Lawrence. So you really can pop down to the Louvre from there. It must be quite the hovel, though.'

'I don't need much. A home is a place to be when you're not outside, surely. It gives me a good excuse to go places.'

'How unusual. Don't ever change that, Lawrence. You are a strange boy. Very strange indeed.'

'No. No, I'm very ordinary.'

'Never say that again, child. You owe me that much.'

Once again her change in demeanour disoriented me. I had done something wrong. She had stayed in the same pose for a long time. The mechanics of it were uncomfortable, but when I stood back and admired her, craning her neck up and breathing out a stream of that sickly smoke, it could not have been more natural.

'I need another drink,' she said. 'I haven't seen anybody. And I need another drink when I haven't seen anybody.'

'And what if you have seen somebody?'

'Then I need another several drinks.'

This made no sense to me. Nonetheless, I followed Élodie to the bar. She asked for another Campari and soda.

'This is getting silly,' I said. 'How many of them do you need?'

'As the occasion dictates.'

'Do you always drink this much?'

'I do when I want to have fun. I don't always want to have fun. Sometimes I want to be damned serious.'

'I don't understand that whole concept of fun.'

'Oh dear,' she said. 'You poor lamb. It's worse than I thought.'

She waited for me to explain myself. At a nearby table a woman shrieked with laughter. I watched the barman as he shook a martini, determination written on his face. He would go home after work to a family in one of those whitewashed villas on the outskirts of town. He had a life and a purpose.

'I would rather make my own fun than follow some-one else's,' I said in a single breath.

'Now that I can understand,' Élodie said. 'Why not make me your fun?'

'Because you would enjoy it more than I would.'

'I'm not so sure about that.' She flicked her eyelids up and down, reaching around to straighten her hair. Her elbow was red and flaky. 'Oh hell. Have another drink.'

'I'm all right, thanks.'

'I insist. You might need it if we are to see Ed Selvin again.'

'What if I don't want to see him again?'

'You didn't like him?'

'No.'

There was no point in pretending otherwise, and Élodie deserved to taste her own flavour of bluntness.

'That's a real shame,' she said. 'He's a nice fellow. You don't like him because he is confident, sure of himself. Is that right?'

'What? No, I never said that.'

'It's the most obvious thing in the world. Does he perhaps remind you of the children at school who looked down on your modesty and earnest studiousness with contempt? The ones who thought that you took it all too seriously, and mocked you for that reason?'

'I don't know where you're getting this from,' I scoffed. 'I was happy in school. You wouldn't know. You know nothing about me.'

'But they were right,' she continued, ignoring my growing frustration. 'You do take things too seriously. Have you never wanted to simply relax and love life for what it is? Now, what will you have?'

There was no way to refuse her. I asked the barman for a dry martini.

'You really are a bully,' I said. 'Are you happy now?'

'You've gone to the other extreme, silly boy. You are mixing rum and gin. A true recipe for disaster.'

'You're impossible to please, aren't you?'

'I'll be pleased if you don't end up passed out on the

beachfront. Drinking needs to be treated with sophistication and sensibility. So don't have the whole thing at once.'

'That's not the sort of advice I would expect from you.'

'Well remember it, boy. Retain your dignity.' She picked up her handbag. 'Please excuse me. Won't be a minute.'

I was left to the sound of ambient chat. I always preferred to stand up at the bar, where I had a vantage point of the rest of the room. This was a good bar, made from polished oak and bound by brass. My reflection stood out in the mirror, which had bottles of gin and whisky stacked in front of it, and my head appeared between them. I was becoming sick of the gold. The room was lit to accentuate the yellow end of the hue, and it felt like being stuck behind a pair of tinted glasses. The chandeliers gave off a nauseating glow, and the diamonds were not so much glinting as fading into the half-light.

'Your martini, sir.' The barman had presented it to me on a tray. He wore a mauve tie that set him apart from his customers.

'Thank you.'

He stared at me while pretending to clean down his work surface.

'Is there something else?' I asked.

'No sir, of course not.' He said this in English. My accent must have been worse than I thought. 'Only that your friend is very…How do you say?…Forthright?'

'Forthright. Yes, you could say that.'

'She used to come here a lot.'

It was my turn to stare.

'I have served her many times,' he continued. 'Normally I would not remember, and I am sure that she does not remember me. Always the Campari and soda, though.'

'Right.' I could see Élodie returning from the bathrooms, with her hair rearranged. I bent in closer across the bar. 'Should I be worried about her?' I asked in a conspiratorial sort of a whisper.

'I would not trust her. Be careful, sir.'

She arrived before I could respond. The barman kept watching us out of the corner of his eye. I asked Élodie if we should find a table. We took one by the window and I chose the seat with its back to the bar.

'Are you all right, Lawrence?' she asked. 'You've gone pale. Paler than usual, I mean. Did you not tan at all in Madrid?'

'I never tan. It's an unfortunate constitution.'

'I do feel sorry for you sometimes. No matter—surely some successful men have been pale.' She was trying to think of an example, and failing. Not that it offended me. I had decided long ago that if my pallor meant that I could not go outside very much, at least I could read a lot. But I was not going to relate any of this to Élodie.

'When did you come here last?' I asked.

She put her arms in a triangular formation and leant her head against her hands. I could see the hint of her breasts for the first time, protruding from the purple satin dress. I must have been drunk because I thought of Titian's *Venus of Urbino*, except that Élodie was merely teasing me with her breasts, withholding them. I wanted to touch them.

'A few years ago,' she said. 'Why do you want to know that?'

'Just curious. This isn't one of those places where you would go on a whim.'

'Oh, my whims are never rational. Have we not come here on a whim?'

'That's true, when you put it like that. But who were you with last time?'

Élodie was bemused. She slanted her brow and shook her head, so that the diamond earrings swayed to and fro.

'Why are you asking me these impertinent questions?'

'Surely it's your turn now.'

'Ha. I see. Because you are so unguarded with your thoughts and feelings, you presumed that I would be the same.'

This was unfair, but I could not have said why. I sampled the martini. It was too bitter, without any of the daiquiri's sweetness. I gave a little hiccup.

'I'm sorry, Élodie,' I said once I had recovered. 'I was only wondering. Is there any harm in that?'

'Maybe not. Ask me again when I've had a few more drinks.'

I could feel the alcohol forming a pool in my stomach. I needed water, but there was none available. The bar might as well have been in the Fourth Circle of Dante's *Inferno*.

'Am I allowed to ask about your husband?' I said.

'If you must.'

'Do you love him?'

'How do you define love, Lawrence? This will be a laugh, I am sure.'

There were too many ways to define love. Sophie and I had discussed it during our holiday in Madrid, sitting in a café where the couple at the next table were kissing. The memory of this conversation brought with it a tinge of shame. We had both decided that there were too many different types of love to encapsulate one definition. And so we had searched it up in the dictionary on her phone.

'Devoted affection and union, I guess,' I said, recalling what the dictionary had told us. 'Is there much more to it than that?'

Élodie's eyes opened wider than usual. I could see the slight blemish in her mascara. I realised that I was playing to her expectations. It was as though I were a circus act, giving her the entertainment that she craved.

'Now that is completely limp,' she said. 'Did you steal it from a clergyman?'

'All right, I have to concede that I don't have my own definition of love. That wasn't my question, though.'

'You have never been in love, Lawrence, so you wouldn't know. Shall we say that I love him by my own definition of the word? He is a large part of my world. One day you will understand what I mean by that. Sadly it isn't something that can be explained easily.'

'And yet you're perfectly happy to be unfaithful.'

She snorted, rather an unpleasant noise, and I hoped never to hear it again.

'Faith? I have never come across a sillier idea. If I devoted the whole of my life to one person, then wouldn't you think that rather a dull life?'

'I suppose so.'

'No, Lawrence, you don't *suppose* anything. Either yes or no. Which is it?'

Her eyes flitted around while she spoke. She never lingered. I must have given much more away with my eyes. They were always open and waiting to be caught. I had not thought about it before. It was intimidating to sit across from her, now that our faces were on the same level.

'I don't know,' I said at last. 'I can imagine fidelity working for most people.'

'But not me.'

'How can you know if you've never tried?'

'Oh, I have tried.' She said this in a defensive way, as

though she had been expecting the question. She previewed everything somehow, like a clairvoyant. 'Your failures in adulthood might be easy to guess, but rest assured that mine aren't.'

'That's very reassuring.'

I had been about to say something else, but I held back.

'We must get some dinner,' she said. 'Or are you feeling the effects of that revolting bouillabaisse?'

'Not really.' This was a lie, and she must have seen it. 'You don't like to stay in one place for long, do you?'

'Not if I can help it. We miss out on an awful lot if we stay in one place. Who knows what might be going on elsewhere?'

She stood up, and I needed no persuasion to abandon my martini. She drew into the light beneath a chandelier, and I had to marvel at how smooth her skin was from this particular angle. It took on an even more lustrous gold.

'You look beautiful, by the way,' I said. She smiled at me in her usual mischievous way. As we walked past the barman's field of vision, I tried to avoid him.

7

The decor in the hotel's restaurant was in keeping with everything else. I was becoming accustomed to the excess. There were three layers of linen on each table. I took issue with the china plates, which were decorated with violent pink roses. The waiter had to ask twice before I gave him my coat.

We sat at an angle next to each other, close to touching. Élodie ordered a bottle of Bordeaux that was not even the most expensive on the menu, and I told her so once the waiter had left.

'The most expensive wine is not usually the best,' she said. 'It depends on what you want out of the wine. The waiter would disagree. That is another point, in fact. The waiter does not always know best. I should start writing all this down for you.'

'I'm sure I can remember,' I said dryly.

She hit me with her napkin in a way that I never could have without somebody noticing.

'This is all useful. One day you might impress a girl with it.'

I had to wonder what sort of a girl would be impressed by any of this. Did she mean Sophie? The dining room was impressive, but only in the way that Albert Speer's architecture was impressive. It was an enormous construction of nothingness, a fantasy created for those with enough money to pay for its upkeep. Anybody could have been impressed by it, although it would be difficult to love.

The wine arrived with a decanter, and the sommelier used a silver breath-easy and a muslin cloth. He held the decanter up to a candle. It could have been a scientific experiment. The process took too long, and the formality of it was unbearable. The waiter went to pour me a tasting glass, but Élodie interrupted and insisted on trying it herself.

'I am sorry about that,' she said, once we were alone. She did not sound at all sorry. 'But I could not have you making a fool of yourself with the wine. You are playing a role now, and we must stick to it.'

'And what role is that, exactly?'

'Do use your imagination,' she snapped. 'I would hate for people to think that you are my son.'

'Like Ed did.'

'He didn't really. There is no need to take him seriously. But I think that you could pass for somebody much older, if you made the effort.'

'So let me taste the wine.'

'Not until you understand what it means to taste. You are in the real world now.'

I swirled my glass and drank. The wine's bouquet was lifeless and the tannins stuck to the corners of my mouth. It tasted old and faintly rotten. It was anticlimactic to think that this, the first truly expensive wine that I had ever tasted, could be so bland. If this were the real world, then even the real world had to be imaginary on some level.

But I did not pursue this thought; my mind was beginning to numb. I regretted the second cocktail. The room was pulled into a wide angle, and the golden light softened at the edges.

Élodie ordered the degustation menu. I had wanted the à la carte, unaccustomed as I was to the obscure gourmet dishes. But she knew what she was doing. Besides, the French menu was too difficult to decipher.

'What sort of films were you in?' I asked.

'Not very good ones,' she said. 'I was in a couple of those eighties, neo-noir pictures. Bad crime flicks, very Los Angeles. No reason a smart boy like you should have heard of them. They were terrible, really. But they gave me an excuse to go to the right parties, to meet the right people.'

'And was Ed Selvin involved in them?'

'No. I never did anything with Ed. We move in different circles.'

'What sort of circles does he move in?'

'More highbrow. His last project was some sort of an art-house thing set in Japan. Shinto imagery and gratuitous encounters. I can't claim to have seen it.'

'So what is he doing here?'

'That girl. They might just have married. Hence the desire to get away from us.'

I tried to conceal my surprise. He had never introduced her. I had always thought that newlyweds were determined to show one another off.

Élodie grew resentful as she talked about Vanessa, but she quickly changed the subject. The entrées came plated extravagantly, and I tried to stop myself from eating too fast. Élodie turned her nose up at the first mouthful and put her cutlery down.

'This place isn't what it used to be,' she muttered. 'It is disturbing to think that haute cuisine might be becoming a tourist attraction. Look at these people. Tourists.'

It was true that some of our fellow diners had played reluctantly to the dress code. I became more satisfied with my navy blue jacket and my white trousers. I decided that they were in fact exceedingly stylish; they suggested success. They set me apart from the tourists. I could pretend that all of this was familiar to me, that I had seen it a hundred times. Was that snobbish? Sophie would have told me so. She would have teased me about these clothes. Or she would have been mortified. The more I thought about it, the less sure I was of what she would think.

'Isn't that true of Paris, too?' I said. 'I can't find a good restaurant anywhere in my area.'

'Give it time. I will show you the best of the best in Paris. It helps if you have some money, of course.'

'I thought you said that the best wasn't necessarily the most expensive.'

'Well remembered,' she said briskly, as though I had wound a key in her back. 'It all depends on whether you want the best food or the most authentic food. Authenticity hardly exists in Paris. But I know of places that have yet to be plundered by the Americans and the Brits, places where they have no English menu.'

'This isn't bad, of course.'

'It could be worse. But please don't eat so fast.' I had cleaned my plate, spooning up every last morsel. 'Christ, this is what having children must be like.'

'You never wanted children?'

'No. I would have made a terrible mother. Besides, the day that a woman gives birth is the day that her life as she knew it ends. I've always been happy with it like this.'

I was about to ask her why she was so happy to live

out this fantasy, but I stopped myself. I would have to be subtler.

'Who are your parents, Lawrence?' Élodie asked after the entrées had been cleared. I thought about what to tell her, if anything.

'They are both lawyers, and they have been doing the same thing for years. But I don't want to talk about them. We don't get on very well.'

'So you are casting off into Europe on your own. How Byronic of you. Tell me more. What do they think of all this travelling business? They must have other plans for you.'

'I'm sorry,' I said, avoiding her and fiddling with my cutlery in the hope that she would stop interrogating me. 'Ask me anything else.'

I waited for her to persist, but to my surprise she backed off.

'All right. But if you do want to talk about it, then I can be an impartial ear.'

'I don't trust that.'

'What? My ability to remain impartial?'

'Well, yes.'

'That doubt is well-placed, Lawrence.'

Rather than waiting for the sommelier to return, she leant over to pour me another glass of wine. I could see the pale skin on the inside of her arm.

'Isn't that my job?' I asked.

'Indeed it is. You must be learning. Go on, pour me a glass.'

I did so, and in the process I managed to send drips over the linen tablecloth.

'Oh well,' she said, 'at least you had the right idea. Women love a man who takes initiative. They will forgive you all sorts of sins.'

'But it's dull chivalry, isn't it? Mindlessly following a set of conventions. I think that women might be after something else these days.'

'What, like your girlfriend? She isn't one of those earnest little feminists, is she? Does she take offence every time you hold the door open for her?'

'I wasn't talking about her.'

'You were. And it isn't true. Even the diehard feminists want their men to be little princes. Don't let anybody tell you otherwise. It is human nature.'

The sommelier returned to retrieve the decanter. He had the wine list, and he was about to present it to Élodie when I held out my hand.

'I'll take this one,' I said. Even the list of dessert wines was overwhelming. Élodie looked over my shoulder as I read it, but I kept it to myself. I asked for a Sauternes. It was not the most expensive, though the price was outrageous for such a small bottle.

'Well done,' Élodie said when the sommelier left. 'I am

impressed. How did you guess my favourite dessert wine?'

'Beginner's luck.'

This did not convince her.

'All right,' I said. 'If you must know, I saw you looking at a bottle of it at the bar. Wistfully.'

'I don't believe that. Where did you gain these powers of observation, Lawrence? They could be put to much better use.'

This time I insisted on tasting the wine. I did not make a fool of myself. She watched me smugly as I swirled the glass and sniffed just as she had.

The courses continued to be delivered, and Élodie picked at her food while I made sure to eat it all. She did not want to linger in the restaurant after the third dessert course, and she left a paltry tip.

'I want to find Ed again,' she said. 'He is always up for a good time. I could do with some fun now.'

'I'm not enough fun for you?'

She surveyed me as though she were a performance assessor, and I her hapless employee.

'No,' she said. 'You may be many things, Lawrence, but you are not much fun.'

She went to return indoors, and I followed hesitantly. It felt like a bizarre old-fashioned farce, where I was a fusty chaperone pursuing my lady around the grounds of a dangerous social gathering. She was heading for the reception desk, and I ran to catch up with her, even though she was the one wearing high heels. She asked the concierge to connect her to Selvin's room.

'Ed, darling,' she said into the telephone. I changed my assessment: she did sound drunk. 'Do come down here. I don't care what you're doing. It's damned antisocial. Join us for another drink.' He said something in response to this, and she shrieked with laughter. 'Oh Ed, you naughty man. I know exactly what you mean. No, that will come later. I'm not as impatient as you are, and he certainly isn't. Come downstairs, you dirty old man. We're waiting for you in the bar.'

The concierge tried to hide his amusement. He too could have seen Élodie before. She must have left the same imprint on everybody. Hanging up the phone, she beckoned for me to follow her through to the bar, which was quieter than before. It was becoming dark outside, and guests were heading to dinner after their aperitifs.

'If only this hotel had a casino,' she said, having ordered yet another Campari and soda. I asked for iced water this time. 'Then we could really have some fun. Say, there's an idea. Why don't we go to the one down the road?'

'So now you want to gamble your husband's money?'

'Why not? I have nothing to lose.'

'That's not a good idea, Élodie. You could end up in trouble.'

'I could. One day you will learn to appreciate the joys of danger.'

The alcohol should have induced a sense of euphoria, but I was not feeling it. I wondered if what it gave to one person it took away from another. Élodie was becoming my responsibility, and this made me anxious. A few hours ago she had been an image of adulthood, and now she was a pouting child. I was dreading another confrontation with Selvin.

'You're so tense, boy,' Élodie observed. At least she had quietened down. 'Why don't you have another drink? It might help you get on with Ed a little better.'

I didn't want to get on with Ed a little better. I wanted to tell Élodie that she was being unkind, and that I would rather go up to the suite, while she hung off the bar and drank with Ed. She reached out to take her drink from the barman, and I noticed the underside of her arm again. There were a few hairs in the sphere of her armpit that she must have missed. I imagined her putting that arm around me and pulling me closer, pushing her breasts up to me. And then I imagined her doing the same thing with Ed, and I decided that I needed to stay because I did not want him to take her from me.

I ordered another daiquirí. It was a different barman. The other one had disappeared. Perhaps his shift had ended, and he was cycling home through the dark. The drink tasted sweeter this time. The new barman must have put more sugar in it.

'Where the hell is he?' Élodie muttered. 'I can't stand this waiting. I might have to get properly drunk if he takes much longer.'

'Please don't.'

'I will do as I please, you silly boy. You are too young to understand what this means to me.'

'So tell me what it means.'

Before she could answer my question, I saw that Selvin had come through to the bar. He looked livelier than before, and he grinned at us in a way that seemed to be saying something else entirely.

'How are we, kids?' he said. 'Vanessa's not feeling too well. She might come down later.'

'No matter,' Élodie said in a dismissive way. 'Have a drink. Did you have dinner up in the room?'

'I did. We did. How was yours?'

'It would have been wonderful if there weren't so many tourists around here. I used to love going out to dinner, but how can I enjoy it when I have to share it with them?'

'You used to be so enthusiastic about things like that,' Selvin said, mockingly wistful. 'What happened? I miss the old Élodie.'

'She's dead,' she said, and they both found this

amusing. It must have been another in-joke. 'Come on, darling, have a drink.'

He asked for a cocktail that neither the barman nor I had ever heard of, and he had to explain that it consisted of Pernod and coffee liqueur. He grinned again, and this time he directed it at me.

'Still on the same daiquirí, huh kid?'

I considered leaving again. Neither Ed Selvin nor Élodie had welcomed me into this conversation—they might as well have been on their own. But I told myself to be patient, and to withstand Selvin's company in the hope that Élodie still wanted me. This suspicion was confirmed as she asked the barman for more champagne and foie gras to be delivered up to the suite in an hour, while Selvin went to find a table. Resolving to follow their lead, I reinforced my smile and armed myself with the cocktail glass.

8

Élodie continued to drink enthusiastically, while I treated my cocktail with more caution. My mouth was drying up. But I felt compelled to quench it by drinking more. I could see why Élodie had fallen into this trap. A chilled cocktail was more refreshing than a glass of water.

Selvin somehow managed to keep himself composed, despite the potency of his liquid death. I could smell it from the other side of the table, and it was a cloud of mismatched flavours. He and Élodie were talking about Vanessa who, true to her prediction, was indeed his newfound bride. It made me think that something was amiss if she stayed in the suite while he had a drink with a female friend.

'How did you meet?' Élodie asked in a voice that did little to mask her bitter anticipation. 'I demand all the details, or I will have to punish you.'

'We met on the shoot for *The Hollow Cave*. She was a

last-minute casting choice. Her predecessor was involved with the scripting, so we had to throw her in at the deep end. It became a little less than professional. She's one hell of a minx.'

'I can imagine. Are you hopelessly in love with her, silly man?'

'She works for me. Like how you work for Marcel. Or is it the other way around? I can never remember.'

Élodie's expression froze, with her mouth half-open and her teeth showing. I was reminded of a Modigliani painting, in which the subject's long face and vacant stare suggested her disapproval.

'Lawrence, do tell Ed about your studies in art history. It must be fascinating.'

Normally, I would have relished this conversation starter, but now it felt as though my every word was being judged. I started in on the rivalry between Ingres and Delacroix, which I had been reading about. Ed nodded along like a bored parent.

'Boy, that sounds interesting,' he drawled. 'So what are you hoping to do with your degree?'

'I never really set out with a plan. I just want to do something that interests me.'

'Fair enough, kid. You're young. Hell, I didn't know what I was doing until I hit thirty. Then I decided to turn my life around. And look where I am now.'

'Well, we're both here,' I said. He ignored me. I wondered what my role was in this conversation, if I even had one. He and Élodie continued to talk without me. I excused myself to the bathroom.

The table was near to the doorway, separated by a pillar, and I realised that I could hear them from the other side of it. I drew in close, so that I would not be standing in the way of the waiters, and tried to make out what they were saying. They were laughing, and it took them a while to recover.

'Who the hell is that guy?' Selvin asked.

'I don't know,' she said dismissively. 'He's a project. I wanted to have some fun if I had to be stuck here. Trust me, if I had known that you were going to be here then I wouldn't have bothered.'

'And what about Marcel?'

'*What* about Marcel? Darling, you know what I should do. I will kick my way out if I have to.'

'You probably won't get a chance. How do you think he will react when he finds out what you've been doing?'

'It really doesn't concern me. How will Vanessa react when she finds out about me?' She drawled the name, as though it was the most absurd that she had ever heard.

'She won't.'

'But you want her to. You want another excuse to escape.'

'You flatter yourself.'

'And yet it is an attractive prospect, wouldn't you say?'

'It sure is,' he said. 'But I need to know that I can trust you. I need to know that you won't go running off with the project, or whatever the hell he is. It's no way for a woman of forty-five to behave.'

'Oh Ed, don't pretend you know how old I am. But don't worry. The last thing that I need is another lovelorn puppy hanging off my arm.'

I decided to leave. Surely I was more than that? Surely she saw more in me? I recalled what she had said about potential in the taxi. She could have changed her mind. She might never have made up her mind about me. And she could say whatever she wanted about me when I was gone and I would never have to hear it. I took a step towards the exit.

But then I stopped myself. Biarritz was no less alien than Hendaye. There was nowhere to go in the night with no money. I thought about sleeping on a park bench, clinging to my suitcase and waiting for the sunrise. That would be a bitter dénouement. And Élodie would keep playing to this script without me. I wanted to see where it would take me, if I were to keep acting out this role that may or may not have been written for me. There were no other lavish film sets in this town. There was only the park bench.

These thoughts drove me to abandon my hiding place,

even though the timing was wrong. I returned to the table. Élodie continued to talk as if nothing had happened, while Selvin was tense and unhappy about being interrupted.

'That was fast,' she said. 'We were discussing your fascinating account of... What was it? *Le Violon d'Ingres*?'

'Something like that.'

The two of them might as well have been a married couple, and me their unwanted child. Selvin's cheeks were flushed and veiny. His eyes were tired but not kind.

'Say, I fancy a smoke,' he said. 'You like cigars, kid?'

'Can't say that I do.'

'He's never tried one before,' Élodie said, 'so he wouldn't know. I say it's a fabulous idea. We can have our drinks outside.'

The terrace was dark and quiet, although there were some people at the poolside tables. I could hear the waves breaking on the beach, but I couldn't see them. Illumination came only from the bulbs set into the swimming pool and the restaurant terrace beside it. Across the beach, the lights of the town's taller buildings glinted like crystals on black velvet.

Selvin had his cigars in a pocket-sized humidor, which was sleek and had a cutter fastened to the lid's interior alongside a thermometer. He held one out to me.

'No, really, I don't think I will,' I said.

'Come on, Lawrence,' Élodie said in drunken

exasperation. 'You can't dismiss it without trying it at least once. You don't inhale these, so they are healthier, if that really worries you.'

I had decided to stay. I would smoke the cigar, to discover how it felt. I took the brown finger. It had the texture of flaky skin. I pretended to know what I was doing with the cutter, and I took too much off. I tried to think of the times I'd seen this elaborate process in films, and I puffed heavily as Selvin held up the lighter. I felt the thin first wave in my mouth.

'I'll regret this tomorrow,' Élodie said. 'It always feels as though a family of gypsies has paraded through my mouth.'

'Are you kidding?' Selvin said. 'This taste is as good as they get. It's sex in the mouth.'

I tried to keep my coughs and splutters under control as I breathed in the smoke and it clouded and swirled.

'What do you think, Lawrence?' Élodie asked.

'Not bad.' My voice sounded nothing like its old self. It had aged several years. 'Rather strong.'

'Twenty years I've been smoking these,' Selvin said, 'and I've never heard anyone describe it like that before. Either you love it or you hate it. Nobody has ever held such a bland view of a Montecristo.'

'Well, I'm the first at something for once.'

Élodie must have seen how much distress I was in.

I wanted to throw first the cigar and then myself over the parapet.

'You don't need any more than that,' she said. 'Put it out if you don't like it.'

'Hey, I'm not having that,' Selvin said. 'Men finish their cigars. Learn to enjoy it.'

I sought relief from my daiquirí. Somehow it had become the more attractive option. My head felt light. I was even more desperately in need of water. I took another puff.

'Give it here,' Élodie said. She left it to smoulder in the ashtray. 'You did well for a first time. It gets easier with each experience.'

'Some people never experience these sorts of things.'

'And good riddance to them.'

It amazed me that Élodie could be so intimate one minute and so cold the next. She was everywhere and she was nowhere. I wanted to feel as though we were the two most important people in the world again, as we had been in the restaurant, discussing her favourite wine and pouring it for each other. If only there could be one Élodie, the one that I imagined lying beside me on the beach, her hair wet and salty, her eyes alive with longing. Now I could not see her eyes because they were directed at Selvin.

Music started to come through the outdoor speakers. It was a mid-tempo bossa nova with a wispy saxophone.

'Good Lord,' Élodie said. 'How do they do that? They

somehow guessed that I was in the mood for a dance right about now.'

'This is what we pay them for,' Selvin said. 'I'll sit this one out, though.'

'Too bad. What about you, Lawrence? You could give me a preview of your moves.'

'A preview?'

'Do I really have to explain everything? Come and dance with me.'

She had asked Ed first. That was enough to make me resist the temptation.

'Sorry,' I said. 'I'm a terrible dancer.'

'Very well, gentlemen. I will give you both a demonstration.'

She moved to the centre of the terrace, backlit by the restaurant and the swirling blue hue of the swimming pool. They cast her into a silhouette. She moved in time with the music, and gave her whole body over to it. Her figure became an extension of the sound.

I was mesmerised. Her hips drew in and out, her limbs became liquid. She flowed along her own channel, and she closed her eyes as she spun around with her arms out wide. It was an act of abandon, yet somehow she kept her dignity.

Selvin applauded once the song had ended, as did a few others who had gathered on the other side of the swimming pool to watch her. I did not. Time had slowed.

I could feel the day's decaying warmth waiting to be swept off by an Atlantic breeze. Élodie took an exaggerated bow to the audience in her self-made theatre.

'It really is exhausting,' she said, returning to us.

'Where in the hell did you learn how to dance like that?' Selvin asked.

'Copacabana. You know, that old cliché. Don't you remember? I lived there for a while.'

'Of course I remember.' He grinned at her in a knowing way. 'Back when it was the place to be, right?'

Their discussion was of little interest to me. Élodie's vitality now filled her to the brim. I was in awe of her. There was something particularly beautiful about the way that she smoked her cigar. She craned her neck in a swan-like arc, allowing the smoke to stream out of her mouth, neither too fast nor too slow. There was a surreal quality to her performance. I could have watched it forever.

9

Selvin excused himself, saying he was going to check on Vanessa. Perhaps she really was ill. Élodie watched him stride away.

'Why don't you dance, Lawrence?' she asked.

'I don't know. It doesn't come naturally to me. You were extraordinary, by the way.'

'Don't feign enthusiasm. It always fails to impress me.'

'I wasn't feigning anything.'

'Oh darling, you don't have to be earnest about absolutely everything.'

I finished my drink, in a weak effort to wash away the remnants of smoke hanging on my breath.

'How are you feeling?' she asked. I swayed my head from side to side as if to say, *so-so*. She bent in closer. We were sitting at one of the tables by the parapet, facing towards the hotel, which loomed above. I could see our suite and the terrace with the light streaming out through the open doors.

The stars were already coming out. The stars never came out in Paris. The last time I had seen them they had been hanging over an open field in New Zealand. It felt healthy to be able to see them now.

'Shall we abandon Ed?' Élodie continued. 'I get the feeling that he won't be coming back.'

'That depends. Am I still your lovelorn puppy?'

Her face remained an unopened envelope.

'I thought that you might have been listening. Bear in mind that what I say to Ed is not necessarily how I feel.'

Once again I felt a violent urge to walk away. Why had I spent my afternoon and evening with her?

'Christ,' I said. 'It really is all about appearances with you, isn't it? Are you ashamed of me?'

'Not particularly. I just think that you need more work. We've done well so far, though.'

'And what is the truth? Am I supposed to guess how you feel about me?'

Élodie ignored the question. She disappeared into the shadows.

'We don't have to take things too fast,' she said without warning.

'No?'

She grew flustered. 'Well, it's true that we already have,'

she said. 'Point taken. But you shouldn't feel any obligation.'

'I don't. I would hate to take any of this too seriously.'

'Oh good. You are learning.'

Our chairs had moved closer together somehow. She reached around my middle, feeling my abdominals as though she was trying to reach beneath my skin and exhume them.

'Interesting,' she said. 'Very interesting.'

I could not have resisted her grip, even if I had tried. She moved up to my chest and rubbed it. I could feel her trying to get beneath the buttons of my new shirt. She burrowed her head into the curve of my neck, and I smelt her hair, which was thick with the scents of smoke and lavender.

'What are you doing?' I asked, trying not to gasp. I had no way of responding to her touch.

'I'm unwinding you, I hope. Relax and let it happen.'

'No.' I pulled away. Her face was half-lit, which made it hard to tell if she was displeased.

'I wanted to see how you would react,' she said. 'You were mine for a while there.'

Suddenly I saw that this really was no more than a joke. That moment was meant to have happened with Sophie. Why had we never touched each other in that way? Why had we sat so far apart on the café terrace in Madrid and discussed the meaning of love from such an intellectual perspective? Why had I talked about Goya's *La Maja Desnuda* without once mentioning the shape of her breasts or the hint of her pubic hair? I had a sudden sense of how I had let Sophie down, what a stitched-up creature I was with her. That was where I needed to return. I needed to save myself for Sophie.

'I'm going up to the suite,' I said. 'I need to sleep. I need to figure out what I'm going to do with myself tomorrow.'

I headed for the steps leading to the hotel, stumbling on the tiles. The terrace was empty, although there were some patrons in the poolside restaurant.

Before I could reach the steps, she called out. 'If you don't come back, Lawrence, then I will throw myself in the water and probably drown. Do you want that?'

She sounded as serious as a drunkard could. I didn't know how to react. The answer to her question was obvious. But it was her problem, and she wasn't my responsibility.

'Whatever, Élodie.'

It was too late and I was too tired. I returned to my path, passing into the light and starting up the canopied steps. The splash did not come until I had reached the top. I turned around to see a purple satin dress billowing out in the water, consuming her tiny figure.

This time I did know how to react. I ran down the steps to the water's edge, peeling off the navy jacket and shirt before I dived in after her.

The water was surprisingly warm, almost leisurely. Surely I should have been rescuing my beloved from the bottom of an ice-cold lake? She offered no resistance, and this hardly surprised me. After all, I had given in to her desires.

I began to pull her to the surface when I felt her finger-nails tighten around my wrist as she tried to claw me down with her. I opened my eyes and saw her face right before mine. Her mouth would have been grinning, I felt sure, if it had not been filled with water. She could have pulled me to the bottom of the pool, drowning us there together, sharing our last breaths in panic. But I released myself, and tugged her to the surface.

A crowd had gathered on the terrace, mostly staff from the restaurant. One of them helped us out. Élodie rolled on the tiles beside me and laughed unrestrainedly. I did my best to explain to the waiter that she had drunk too much. This made Élodie laugh harder.

'Come on,' I said, taking her by the arm. 'We need to go up to the room.'

I apologised to the waiters, gladly taking a towel and my clothes from one of them. It all felt too strange to be true. The onlookers were mesmerised. Élodie's dress was ruined. It had drawn in around her, revealing how thin she truly was.

I tried not to let too much water inside the building.

Heads turned as we went past: one bare-chested young man and one drenched older women. It must have been something of a spectacle. Despite the absurdity I joined in Élodie's laughter. We ran up the grand staircase, past an American couple and their children. They shielded the little girl's eyes.

The champagne and foie gras lay waiting on a tray. Feeling the adrenaline, I popped the cork enthusiastically. It hit the ceiling, and I fell onto the bed, sharing in Élodie's high spirits, and drank from the bottle. She kicked off her shoes and undid her dress, which fell to the floor in a lumpy heap.

'Remember to be gentle,' Élodie whispered in my ear as she laid herself over me. Her breath was warm and heavy. 'Don't get too excited.'

This was useless advice. I wasn't at all sure what to do so I followed my instincts, even though they had not served me well up until that point.

'Start with a touch,' she said. I laid my hand tentatively on her thigh. The skin was as smooth as I had imagined it. But Élodie took my hand and dragged it to her breast.

'Up here. I want it here.'

Beneath her guiding hand I could feel the point of her nipple, the firm skin that bound her breasts, and the hint of her ribs. Her grip was as strong as it had been in the swimming pool, her nails digging into my skin.

Then she rolled on her side and directed my hand down between her thighs. I could feel the scar and the moles on her back beneath my fingers and I ran my hands over and over them as I surged, feeling my own strength for the first time. It went on that way for a long time. Our mouths were close, and I could feel the warmth of her panting. She writhed beneath me, tossing and turning as I raced ahead.

'Let's try that again,' she said, once we had both caught our breath. I was still inside her. 'More carefully this time.'

We lost ourselves for what felt like hours. She showed me how to touch her, when to slow down and when to hurry. When I came back into contact with a steady stream of thought, I felt a new sensation coursing through my blood, a combination of terror and euphoria. Part of me wanted to collapse laughing while the other wanted to burst into tears. She lay beside me. We were both exhausted.

'Not bad,' she said. 'Not bad at all. We certainly have material to work with.'

She got up and put on a silk kimono, which she'd found in her suitcase. Then she reached over to the tray and poured two glasses of champagne.

'I really should scold you for drinking from the bottle,' she said. 'But I rather liked it. Very caveman of you.'

We clinked glasses. I was elated. I had shared her body in such a spectacular way. It was a momentous achievement, and yet it was also shocking. Nobody must ever find out about this, I told myself. It was to be my wonderful secret, my dirty dream.

'How was that for a first time?' I asked.

She drew out her bottom lip, as though the answer required some thought.

'You are the only virgin I have slept with, so I can't make an informed comparison. A bit like your cigar smoking, it needs improvement. But it is promising.'

'Were you really trying to drown yourself?' It sounded silly even as I said it. But rather than mocking me she looked up at the ceiling, as though some detail in the patterned plaster had caught her attention.

'I'm not sure,' she said. 'The thing is, I would try anything once to see what happens. Perhaps you know what I mean by that now.'

Élodie excused herself to have a shower. This left me to my disoriented self and a glass of champagne. Something had come over me, and the reality was becoming clear. It had been a febrile madness. I had injected myself with Élodie Lavelle and she had left an infection. Her life was saved and I was her saviour.

Standing before the mirror, I tried to make sense of what happened. I could hear the shower running. She was humming, and this sound made me stare more intently at my naked self with his pointed shoulders and his patchy chest hair. *Who are you?* I asked my reflection.

'You should come and join me, darling,' she called.

I ignored her and put on a dressing-gown. In the main room I reclined on the sofa and ran a hand through my wet hair. Sophie was on my mind again, even as I told myself not to think of her until the morning. None of this would have happened if I had done what she wanted in Madrid. Now I was forever tainted, and I would not see her again for months. What was I going to tell her? Could I tell her anything? It felt as though I had betrayed her twice.

Élodie had left her handbag on the sofa. I wondered if it would be wrong to give in to my curiosity. The handbag was, I knew, any woman's nerve centre. But I felt the allure of it. She must have left it there deliberately. Perhaps it would shed some light on her true self. Or perhaps this was wishful thinking. The shower was still running, so I opened the bag.

A white leather wallet contained cash, Marcel's card, and a few business cards. One was for a limousine service in Paris. Another was for a restaurant in the Fourth that I had never heard of. Somebody had scrawled a telephone number on it. Perhaps because of a simple possessive desire, or perhaps for no good reason at all, I copied the number onto a scrap of paper and pocketed it. The rest was bottles of perfume, make-up, mirrors, and cigarettes. It shed no light whatsoever.

I returned the bag to the sofa. It did not pay to pry, and I had succumbed to yet another temptation. One of many that day. And there was one left. I wrote *Lawrence Williams* and my number on a different scrap of paper and slipped this into her handbag.

My vision was beginning to blur. I tried to walk in a straight line out to the terrace. The air was heavy, but when the wind came in I felt the sea on my cheeks. I tried to remember how we had stood in this very place a few hours ago. It was already a distant memory, when everything had been so much simpler.

'What are you doing out there?' Élodie said from the main room. She was wearing that beautiful dressing-gown, with a sash pulled tight beneath her breasts. I went over to her and wrapped my arms around her waist. She drew in close to me. I could smell her just-washed hair.

'Thank you,' I said. But it was not my voice. She drew back.

'Oh Lawrence. Get yourself to bed. I'll join you in a few minutes.'

I clambered into bed and tried to remember the morning. I had woken at six and not stopped moving. Sophie and I had breakfasted before taking a taxi together to the north station in Madrid. We had waited around on the platform, wondering how to say goodbye—whether to kiss or hug or wave. In the end I had bent over awkwardly to hug her, and she had cried. I had forgotten about the crying. And I had forgotten that she had walked away without replying to my goodbye.

I drew the sheets up around my head. Élodie was in the next room. I heard the clasp of her handbag, and another snap that could have been her pocket mirror. I rolled over and tried not to think about what the next day would hold.

My vision grew dim. I had to sleep, even though I wanted to wait for her. I could smell her in the linen, her clean and understated perfume, along with something that smelt of lavender. Even as I pushed my nose into her pillow I could sense the sweet odours were fading.

10

When I woke the sun was already high and the curtains were shaking in a breeze from the open window. There was no sign of Élodie. My mouth was parched and tasted of smoke and rotting tannins. My lips were swollen.

I staggered into the bathroom. In the mirror my eyelids drooped, even as I tried to open them. I ran the basin full of cold water and kept my head beneath the surface for as long as I could.

The bedroom was a mess. My clothes were strewn over the floor. Élodie had left her dress behind, and it lay on the carpet in a damp purple mound. I put a corner of the fabric to my nose. It smelt of nothing but chlorine. I let it slump into the puddle of water. She had taken all of her luggage. Had she paid for the suite? If not, it would make for an uncomfortable encounter with the concierge.

There was a pile of cash on the side table. She had left a note on top, which said, *For the train*. I turned it over, and then I tried to find another note, or any other reminder of her presence. There was nothing. I counted the money. One hundred euros. It was generous, on top of everything else. The train would cost less. Or was she saying that I was only worth one hundred euros?

I decided to order in breakfast. It would be worth taking advantage, if this was to be my last experience of total luxury. I checked the time as I put the telephone down. Ten o'clock. She had said that her train was to leave in the morning. She must have already gone. She had spent the rest of the night elsewhere, presumably with someone else. The note was a paltry reminder of our day together. Her script was perfectly formed and italic, written with a sharp nib. She must have used her own pen.

The cooked breakfast and pitchers of coffee and orange juice were delivered as per my request. The steward laid them on the terrace, which was bathed in heat. I drank the coffee fast, although it did little to cure the headache. I shielded my eyes behind sunglasses.

I was now charged with the task of finding my own way home. The rail strike would not have ended. Perhaps Biarritz had an airport; I considered asking the concierge. A good concierge found ways to achieve the impossible.

He could find me a train ticket, given how much I was paying to be in the hotel. But then I remembered that I was not paying for it. It was imperative to avoid the concierge and keep what remained of my cool as I left.

So I packed and left in good time. I had to get out of the suite. Its air was heavy and putrid. I decided to assume that Élodie had paid the bill. After all, it was not my responsibility. The hotel had neither my name nor my contact details. I might as well not have been there.

The concierge was on the telephone when I came down the grand staircase. Keeping my pace brisk, I followed a straight line to the revolving door. But just as I was about to walk through I saw Vanessa out of the corner of my eye. She was alone in one of the gilded chairs with a suitcase between her legs. She was crying. I was about to stop and talk to her, but there was resentment in her eyes. That was last night's world. I had to leave it there.

Outside I followed the road west towards the beachfront, only breathing again when I felt safe that the concierge was not pursuing me with a bill trailing behind him. A taxi drove by and I waved it down. There was nothing left to do in this town, which looked different under today's sun. It was windy, and the morning cloud cover was rolling away fast, replaced by thinner and thinner masses. The sunlight seeped in and out. The old buildings cast shadows that were gone again the next minute.

The taxi took a considerable chunk of my bequeathed euros. There was to be no return trip. I would sleep on the concourse if I had to. The Biarritz station was more welcoming than its Hendayan counterpart. The pavement outside was lined with trees and shrubs, and its elegance was well preserved. I joined the queue to buy tickets.

I was finding it difficult to separate what had really happened the previous day from what felt like a dream. I had been dragged along on an adventure to Biarritz with a woman for whom I had never been prepared. I had gone to dinner with her in a grand hotel, dressed like a playboy. Those were the irrefutable facts. And Élodie had certainly jumped into the swimming pool...

That was the last clear image. After that, the memories became hazy and dislocated. It was undeniable that we had made love. We had *made love*. I wanted to say the words aloud, to shout them from the rooftop, because it was true. I was no longer the boy who could never muster the courage to follow his desires. I was the man who slept with beautiful women and drank champagne with them and wore a navy blue jacket and white trousers. Nobody would believe me. Ethan would dismiss it as a joke. He might have loved talking to girls, but he had never done anything like this.

On the other hand, I also wished that none of it had happened. Or that she had at least stayed the night. Clearly

I was nothing but another toy. She would much rather play with Ed Selvin. Would Selvin have jumped into the swimming pool after her? No, I thought: only I could ever be that foolish.

I reached the end of the queue. The ticket hall was echoic. It felt as though I was standing on a stage before those lined up behind me. The ticket officer was a woman this time, and I thought she would be helpful.

'Hello,' I said in French. 'I need to get up to Paris today, urgently. Is there anything?'

'I'm sorry, sir, but there is nothing. All booked out.'

'Okay,' I continued. 'Well, its essential that I get up to Paris today. I have an important meeting.'

'But if you did not book there is nothing to be done.'

'Please,' I said. I sounded unpleasant to my own ear. 'This is very important. There has to be something.'

She stared at her screen and typed while I waited, rapping my fingers on the desk.

'All right, I do have something here,' she said. 'It is the last seat. First class. One hundred and thirty euros.'

I was aware of the queue growing behind me. I presented her with the remaining eighty euros from Élodie's contribution, and twenty that I had withdrawn in Madrid. I counted my coins and found that they amounted to a mere three euros. My hand shook as I laid them on the counter.

'Can I get a discount on the rail pass?'

'Give it here.'

I reached into the front pocket of my suitcase. There was nothing in it. I fossicked, wondering if this were a tasteless joke the gods of travel were playing on me. In desperation I placed the case out on the floor and searched through all of my clothes and toiletries. I returned to the officer's desk without the pass, and now she was neither friendly nor helpful.

'I must have left it somewhere,' I said. 'Can I go and search for it?'

'You may, but I will probably sell this seat if you leave the queue.'

I had tumbled headfirst into a Fuseli canvas, with carnal fantasy replaced by a lady trying to do her job. I turned to the young man behind me, and asked in English if he could lend me thirty euros. He appeared to be an experienced traveller, with his backpack and hiking boots, and I hoped that my distress would attract his sympathy.

'Please,' I begged. 'I will pay you back. But I need this now, very badly.'

The young man took the notes out of his wallet with some reluctance. I gushed a stream of thanks and apologies and sorted out the ticket with the officer. No doubt she and everybody else in the queue were planning my execution.

Shocked by how comprehensively I had lost my

dignity before a group of strangers, I found a seat on the main concourse. The train that I had booked was the last of the day, and it seemed likely that I had indeed procured the last ticket. I would not be in Paris until at least seven o'clock, meaning I would be stuck with tortuous thoughts of Élodie Lavelle until then.

Images of her were playing through my mind. I could still see her dancing on the terrace, with the darkened cityscape as her backdrop. And I could still feel her wet body beneath my fingers, responding to my touch. It felt impossible that such a thing could have happened. And the thought of the truth making its way to Sophie was paralysing. I would have to talk to her that evening, when I made it back to Paris. I could try and tell her the truth, even though it was still indecipherable to me. Or I could lie about why it took me so long to get back from Madrid. I could tell her that I slept in the station in Hendaye. But she would not believe me, because I would not believe myself. I had read somewhere that true liars have full faith and conviction in their narratives.

The young backpacker emerged from the ticket hall. I waved at him as he walked past, and he returned it. He seemed gentle enough. His skin was pale and veiny, and he wore round, wire-framed spectacles.

'Sorry,' the man said in a Birmingham accent. 'I didn't realise you spoke English. I hardly know any French.'

'Oh,' I said. 'Neither did I. Sorry.'

'Not at all. I'm Marcus.'

'Lawrence.'

I got up to shake his hand, and I admired his railroad watch and his beard, which was thick and untended.

'So I take it you booked your tickets in advance?' I said.

'Yes. Good thing I booked it for the two o'clock, otherwise I'd be in trouble. Did you book for one of the cancelled trains?'

'No. It's a long story.'

'Why didn't you go to the airport?'

'There's an airport?'

'It's around the corner. I would have gone there if I hadn't already bought a return. It would have cost less, and they wouldn't have given you an unassigned seat.'

He was right. The seat number on my ticket was blank.

'Damn,' I said. 'So I can't sit down?'

'Not unless there's a free seat in the first-class carriage. I doubt there will be. This isn't the best time to travel.'

'And they charged me a full fare for it. How bloody typical. You know, I don't care anymore. I just want to get to Paris. Where have you been?'

'Went hiking in the Pyrenées. I wanted to follow in Hemingway's footsteps and go fishing in Burguete. And the bullfighting was something else.'

'You went to Pamplona?'

'Yes,' Marcus said, as though he had been itching to talk about it. 'Have you ever been? It is the greatest thing.'

He went on to explain it in detail. It was relaxing to listen without really taking it in. He sat down next to me, slinging his backpack to the ground with strong arms.

'So after all that I was keen to have some time off before returning to the real world. And I thought that I should finish off the Hemingway tour by visiting another of his haunts. You know he gambled in that casino down by the beachfront? I went in and drank whisky and soda in his honour.'

'What do you do in the real world?'

'I teach English to unappreciative teenage boys in Manchester. Good to get away from it all sometimes. What about you?'

'I'm studying art history. Not in the real world yet.'

'As long as you're not doing it to annoy your parents. That was how I ended up studying literature. I keep thinking, How different would it have been if I hadn't wasted my time and lived my life at that age?'

We waited for the train together and I stopped thinking about Élodie. When the train arrived, I joined the queue for the first-class carriages, waving goodbye to Marcus and promising to send him the money I owed him.

I waited until everybody else was on board before taking one of the padded reclining seats. The conductor came around, dressed in the sort of uniform that suggested rank and responsibility. I handed him my ticket.

'No, you cannot sit here,' he said in French. 'You wait until the car is full, then you take the empty seat if there is one.'

I tried to explain myself and asked why I had been forced to pay full fare for a seat that I was not allowed to sit in.

'Welcome to France,' he said in English.

'So when can I sit down?' I asked.

'After Bordeaux.'

'And I have to stand up until then?'

'Yes.'

And so I found myself in the corridor by the luggage racks. At least I had a view. The landscape was already changing as the train moved further away from Biarritz. It made a brief stop in Bayonne before curving away into the countryside. The whitewashed villas were becoming scarcer, changing to the more familiar French stone cottages. The barren Basque country gave way to woodlands, some with autumnal foliage beginning to show through. Then the woodlands disappeared, replaced by industrial estates and motorway overpasses. I wondered where Élodie was now, if she was already in Paris or if she and Ed Selvin were travelling somewhere else together.

I struggled to remain awake. There was a weight in the air, a fatigue that filled the carriage. It would be a few more hours before they released us into the Parisian wilderness. I wanted to be there. Paris was not home, but at least it never changed.

11

The train was passing through Poitiers when I remembered the telephone number. I took the scrap of paper out of my laptop bag where I had thrown it and tried to decide what to do. It was an American number, although I didn't know the area code. It could be anywhere, given Élodie's endless itinerary. I wanted to call it. Whoever answered could perhaps shed some light on the mysterious lady.

I had taken a seat. A lot of people had alighted at Bordeaux and there were no more stops before Montparnasse. Everything was quiet and peaceful in the carriage, and the train had picked up speed now it was on the Atlantique high-speed line. The catenary poles swept past, some of them distinct, some of them in a blur. It was becoming dark outside, the landscape fading.

My thoughts about Élodie were no longer so clear, either. She had treated me so cruelly, so blithely. Yet I could not restrain a fantasy in which she appeared on the train at that moment. I could see her, walking between the carriages and somehow keeping her footing despite the unsteady movement around her, and those ridiculous heels. She would be wearing the white leopard-print dress again—the one that showed her back with its scar and imperfections—drawing on a cigarette and breathing the smoke into my face.

When the train arrived at Montparnasse I had a lump in my throat that I couldn't get rid of. I had not eaten. This was accentuating a hollow in my stomach.

As soon as I got off the train I searched for a bathroom. I ran cold water over my face again, confronting myself in the mirror. Streaks of grime intersected with my image. I rinsed my mouth and told myself that this was the real world, unembellished and bare.

The city was alive as it always was on a warm summer evening. Many people were out and about, and the café terraces on the Rue de Rennes were filled with men and women in sharp suits and dresses. I might as well have been a tourist, with my worn-in travel clothes.

I crossed the road and turned up the Rue de Mézières, which connected to the Place Saint-Sulpice. The orange sky sat between the two mismatched towers of the church. I had never been inside the church, and although my body ached and wanted nothing more than to be fed and rested,

I felt an urge to pause for a few minutes of contemplation.

Inside it was refreshingly cool. Saint-Sulpice was resplendent in its ornamentation, but it was austere enough to give a slight sense of unease. In the middle of the aisle I took in all the sculptures, the cracked stone arches and the marble columns that rose high over the congregation. Thuribles hung from the ceiling, and the scent of flowers and incense wafted through the church. It reminded me of Élodie's scent.

I decided to take a seat, since the thought of going straight to the apartment was not appealing. The wheels of my case resounded in the high-ceiling church. I put it between my legs and allowed my eyes to wander over the surface of everything. There was a monumental white Madonna and Child statue between the marble columns. She cast her eyes down over the congregation, while the child looked up at her inattentive face with a majestic longing. The statue was lit from above and this cast their shadows onto the wall.

The sun was setting behind a cloud, emerging to send rays through the southern row of windows. Light fell on the cracks and crevices in the floor tiles, and I could see the imprint of three centuries in them. I could see myself, too, reflected in the marble. My face was worn and unshaven, and my mouth was downturned.

The light passed away as fast as it had come. Everything

was cast into shadow again. There was an old woman sitting a few rows up from me. Her eyes were closed; she must have been praying. I had never prayed before. Could I pray too, even though I had nothing to pray for? My desires had been realised, and not in the way I had intended. Now fear had taken their place. I closed my eyes.

The congregation dispersed. As I was about to leave with them I noticed a candle holder, which had a few spaces left. I fished for the last few coins in my pocket. I tried to think of a person for whom I could light this candle, and I looked up at the Madonna for guidance. Nobody came to mind, but I lit it anyway. The flame sprang into life as I held the wick out to another and it danced before me.

I walked briskly towards the other end of the Rue Saint-Sulpice. Ethan would have to let me into the apartment if he was not playing a show that night. He specialised in a fashionable revival of New Wave, and he was something of a genius at it. He had a record out on a Swedish label, yet he was a year younger than me. The intercom was broken, and with no security chip I had to call him from the hotel next door. The concierge recognised me from the last time this happened, and he gave me the telephone reluctantly. It was a luxurious hotel, the comfort and polish of which reminded me of Biarritz. I imagined Élodie walking in with her suitcase and asking for the best room, and both of us spending the night here, with more champagne and more caviar, and making love again.

Ethan met me in the lobby, with his unkempt ginger hair and his boyish grin. His eyes glinted in a way that suggested he was always glad to see you, and his arms were big and spread wide to welcome me and help me with my suitcase. He had not shaved once since we had met, and his adolescent beard meandered all over his chin and down his neck. He was wearing his faded Hawaiian shirt and a corduroy jacket that smelled of cigarettes. He used to wear that jacket instead of his blazer, in the days when we were imprisoned at school together, and his old orange Volkswagen was our escape. He sold that car to pay the first instalment of the rent. That had been his only contribution.

'Professor Williams, I presume,' he said, and despite my exhaustion I could not help but laugh. 'You took your time. What happened?'

I didn't know where to begin, or where to end. I mentioned nothing of Élodie, much as I wanted to impress him with the improbable story. Instead I gave him a version which suggested that I had slept on a bench in the Gare d'Hendaye.

'Oh man, I feel for you,' he said. 'I heard about those strikes, and I was wondering. Shame you missed out on the gig last night. The Swedes were there. You remember

Helga, don't you? She bought me a drink afterwards. I wasn't complaining.'

'I don't remember anyone of that name, Casanova. I'm amazed that you do.'

I allowed him to go into every sordid detail. It seemed that Helga had just left. He occupied one side of the living room, and his clothes spread from an open suitcase, his fold-out bed taking up half the room with a rumpled pile of sheets. The corner by the window contained his laptop and keyboard. This was where I had planned to put my writing desk. He had left the window open, and flies were crawling over the dirty dishes. The liquor supplies were depleted. A bottle of gin, which I could remember opening the day before I left, was nowhere to be seen.

'Have you had dinner?' Ethan asked. 'I've already eaten. And there isn't much in the fridge. Haven't gone to the market yet.'

'I'll pick at something. I've run out of cash.' There was no point in asking him for money. He would gladly lend it, but only if he had any.

'Suit yourself. If you don't mind, I'm about to lay some tracks down. It's going to be surreal pop excess. It all builds up from this resonant keyboard line, then climaxes with this looped orchestra sample that lines up with the main riff. You'll love it.'

'No doubt,' I said. 'Are you going to clean this place up?'

'Sorry, man, I have to get this done while the juices are flowing. Maybe tomorrow. By the way, Sophie called a couple of times.'

He disappeared into his headphones. I brought the telephone through to the bedroom, but not to call Sophie.

The number took a while to connect. It rang several times, during which I felt my pulse rate rise. I was venturing into unknown territory.

'Selvin Studios,' said a woman in an American accent, 'how may I help?'

I put the receiver down in shock. This was strange. Had Selvin given Élodie this number in case she wanted to revive her acting career? Or perhaps it was a cover for them to stay in contact without arousing their spouses' suspicion.

I started up my laptop. There were a few emails that had come through since my departure, but I ignored these and made straight for the browser. I typed *Selvin Studios* into the search engine. The screen burst into life with images of tanned women with oversized breasts, bent over and displaying their backsides to the camera. *Starving cougars get their prey* went the description. One of them was rubbing her nipple and looked pleadingly up at the man who stood over her. Another wore lace lingerie and gartered stockings, and I watched as her partner undid the clasps. He reached beneath the fabric and she gave an exaggerated moan. This made me flinch away from the screen and turn the volume down. Was Élodie in one of these videos? I searched for her name, but nothing came up.

Suddenly I felt nauseous, even though this discovery wasn't a surprise. Selvin, after all, had that air to him: a seamy and tyrannical voyeur. This did nothing to abate my humiliation. Was Élodie a porn star? The possibility made more sense the more I remembered of our night together. She must have given me the standard treatment, just without the cameras. I felt indescribably sad.

I closed the site. It was almost funny. What a fine joke for Élodie and Selvin to have played on me. She was nobody. That answered every last one of my questions. I decided then and there to forget Élodie Lavelle, and whatever fetid bag of history she carried with her.

Two of the emails were from Sophie. They both asked where I had got to, and the second one said that she was at the airport in Berlin and she wanted to hear my voice before she left for New Zealand. What was I going to tell her?

Returning to the main room, I overfilled a glass of wine. Ethan insisted on playing me the track that he had finished, and I leant against the dining table to hear all nine minutes of it. He closed his eyes and played along with an imaginary guitar. It was everything wrong with modern music. I told him so, and he was glad to hear it. This made me think of the tune Élodie had danced to on the terrace the previous day, and how cool and unforced it had all been. It was not so long ago, but it felt like an eternity.

Bolstering myself with the wine, I called Sophie on her mobile phone. She answered on the first ring.

'Well hello,' she said. 'Where have you been?'

'Sorry I didn't call. I got waylaid in Hendaye.' The words felt wrong even as they left my mouth. 'The railway unions were on strike.'

'Oh Lawrence, that's awful. I thought something like that must have happened. Are you all right?'

'I'm fine. It was stressful, and I'm tired, but I'm here now.'

'You don't sound fine. Eat something and make sure to get some sleep. They're about to call my flight, so I haven't got long.'

'Sure. I don't have much more to report. But I did want to say I'm sorry that we didn't have a better time in Madrid.'

I could tell that she was about to ask me what I was on about, but she held back.

'There's always another time,' she said. There was a note of reservation in her voice. 'Although I don't think I'll be over there in December. But we can talk about that later. Promise you'll call?'

'Of course I will. And I love you.'

'What was that? The connection is terrible here. Don't worry about it. This call is costing a fortune.'

'All right. Travel well.'

She hung up. I poured myself another glass of wine, in the hope that this one would send me to sleep. I drank it too fast. Élodie would have been quick to reprimand me. But no, I could not think about her, or what she would have done under any circumstance. She belonged to her own curious world, and I had escaped from it.

I spent a while by the window, watching the pedestrians on Rue Saint-Sulpice. And then, as if by accident, I found myself lying on the bed, staring at the ceiling while my vision blurred and whirled. It was a balmy evening, but the fan stayed off and the window stayed closed, because I was stuck to the bed, incapacitated. I had trouble sleeping that night.

Part II

12

A lot can happen over the course of four months, and yet it is just as possible for nothing to happen. University began in September, and while this did provide some distraction, I was haunted by my unplanned holiday in Biarritz. My nostalgia was so profound that I slipped into lethargy. I slept for long hours and inoculated myself with caffeine for what little of the day remained after I had woken up and dressed.

Every day I waited for Élodie to call. Whenever the telephone rang and my pulse quickened it was only ever Sophie on the other end. She would report whatever was going on in New Zealand—the drinks she had with friends that I had forgotten about, and the gossip of their lives. We would discuss the art she was studying, and she would email me her essays to read. I would edit them severely. Sometimes I would send her one of my essays in return, and she would have no suggestions for improvement.

'It's good,' she would say. 'It's really good.' And that would be that.

During this time I accompanied Ethan to his gigs, which were in dank bars over in the Eleventh and the Fifth. He performed solo with his guitar and his keyboard and his laptop and his microphone, wearing sunglasses and purple trousers, and he would command his audience. Sometimes he would remove his shirt and throw it into the crowd. The French worshipped him, and they would all buy him a drink afterwards and fawn over him while I stood off to the side and tried to find somebody else to talk to. Inevitably he would find a girl to bring back to the apartment, and I would be relegated to my bedroom for the rest of the night.

On those rare occasions when we found ourselves alone, without the company of his French artist friends and their outrageous opinions on everything, we were able to drink and talk about philosophy and books as we used to. He knew all the grimy student bars around the Latin Quarter. One in particular served sangria and had a jukebox that played nothing but old jazz songs. It reminded me of Spain. I was glad to spend hours there, listening to Ethan read me his poetry. I asked him what the point of it all was, and he told me that there didn't need to be a point. He expressed whatever was on his mind, and he did not need to justify it.

The rest of my time I spent trying to live like a Frenchman, drinking wine and eating bread and cheese. University required me to spend most of my spare hours reading. Élodie would have been quick to point out that this pastime was designed for such a terrific bore as me. In my imagination, I responded by asking what pastime was designed for such a terrific whore as her. This was perhaps the result of spending so much time in my own company. I tried hard to rid myself of such thoughts, but Élodie haunted me.

Paris returned to its usual bustle as the year went on. I would walk out into the street after a morning of reading, and let the ebb and flow of humanity dictate where I ended up. Sometimes this took me as far as Boulogne, or Montmartre, or down to the Place d'Italie. I remembered Élodie mentioning her pied-à-terre in the Eighth, and I would walk up and down the Boulevard Haussmann, hoping to catch sight of her emerging from a boutique or a gastronomic restaurant with an inconspicuous doorway. Of course, it never happened. There was nobody but a throng of tourists, photographing the Arc de Triomphe on their mobile phones and eating snails and frog legs in overpriced bistros.

I turned twenty-one in November and I pretended that it hadn't happened. Ethan would have insisted on a celebration if he had remembered. Sophie called in the morning and reminded me that her family never celebrated birthdays, in an effort to cheer me up. I told her she should be here in Paris with me. She told me that she missed me and to treat myself to another wander through the Musée d'Orsay. I did not leave the apartment for the rest of the day. I asked myself why I was clinging to Sophie when she was the lone reminder of what I had left behind. It was because I needed a friend, I told myself, and she was a good friend who had loved me for who I was, back in the days when I knew who I was.

The weather cooled in early December, and the grand overcoats and scarves returned to the shop windows. It was more excusable to be badly dressed in the summer, since I could have called myself a tourist at that time. But now, in cafés and bars, I could sense that the locals disapproved of my fraying clothes. I had kept Élodie's acquisitions, but lacked the occasion to wear them. Her scent stayed on the collar of the jacket for weeks. Where had she found such a potent perfume?

So it happened that one day I decided to line up all of my clothing and make an assessment. I went through everything, and decided that they were consistent only in their ragged hemlines and misshapen cuts. 'One simply cannot go around Paris in an oversized brown shirt,' as Élodie might have said. I collected the rags together in a bundle and heaped them in my suitcase. They needed to be replaced. Wallet in tow, I left the apartment.

The shops at this end of Saint-Sulpice were no good. Those that did not have dead flowers inside and white-wash over the windows were cheap and bleak. I walked past the more conventional shops at the western end of the Boulevard Saint-Germain, reasoning that Élodie would disapprove of them too. I waited at the intersection with the Rue Bonaparte and planned my next move. The buildings in the foreground were bathed in shadow, and the Tour Montparnasse at the end of the street reflected the gold of the setting sun. A folk band played outside the church across the road, attracting a crowd.

The shops changed as I walked down the Rue du Cherche-Midi, which was narrow and quiet. An old woman walked by with her papillon, and little boys in suits and ties were hurried along by their nanny. Halfway up the street I came across the right sort of a place, which had no display windows but did advertise menswear, comfortably removed upstairs.

The assistant on the third floor was the master of his realm, and I was an intruder. He wore a low-cut shirt that showed his chest hair and baggy trousers and suspenders. I was out of place here. I began to search through the racks for something that would not make me look like him. He came over to stand behind me.

'Oh my friend,' he said. 'You need help.'

His words made me wonder if I had misunderstood.

I had not, and the next hour was spent in the midst of a flurry of clothing and accessories that I could not fight my way out of. There were no other customers. I was imprisoned with the assistant as he turned me around and then around again, pressing more items into my arms. I might as well have been one of the mannequins.

'This is a miracle,' he said, as I withdrew from the dressing room in a violet cardigan and a tight pair of jeans. 'You have the perfect body for everything.' He could not contain his excitement, and he clapped his hands as he searched through the racks for yet another combination. 'Has nobody ever told you this before? Well, hear it from me. You are an object of envy, young sir.'

By the time he had finished revising my wardrobe, satisfied that I could be seen in public again, he collected the items together in a pile and followed me down the staircase.

The female voices on the first floor were heated. I paused on the corner of the staircase as I recognised one of them: a lightning-fast, confident French tongue with the accents accentuated and the Rs rolled. I stopped breathing.

'This is an illegal policy,' she said. 'I bought this two weeks ago. Therefore I should be able to return it, since it does not fit.'

The shop assistant tried to explain something, but

Élodie must have thrown her arms up. She clicked her heels across the tiles. I stood rigid, halfway up the stairs. She wore a woollen overcoat, which did not flatter her frail figure in the same way that her summer dress had, but the jewellery and the make-up were there. Her skin had lost all of its radiant tan, and it was a Hellenic shade of white. She paused at the doorway, putting on a pair of sunglasses even though it was overcast. Her head drew up and our eyes were briefly brought together. I stood paralysed, waiting for her to react. But before I could begin to move, she pushed the sunglasses down like a visor and strode into the crowded street.

My first impulse was to run after her. But she had walked away too fast, and I needed to pay for the clothes.

'Who was that woman?' I asked the assistant at the counter.

'She demanded to return the dress that she bought here two weeks ago. We have a strict no-returns policy. Why do you ask? Do you know her?'

'I thought I recognised her. Perhaps not.'

'She is old enough to be your mother.'

I laughed at this, in such an airy way that I could have been Élodie. The male assistant wrapped my new acquisitions in white paper, all the while explaining what a stroke of good luck my presence had been.

The female assistant took my credit card. 'There aren't many men who could do that,' she said with something close to sincerity. 'Have you ever considered modelling?'

'No, I haven't. I'm not the type.'

'You most certainly are. You should think about it. Male models are always needed in this city.'

I excused this as her attempt, however flattering, to validate the sale.

All faces were replaced by Élodie's as I walked up the Rue de Rennes. They were impossible to ignore, all judging me in much the same way that she had, as though I were a bad memory that needed to be repressed. I shuffled past them all. It had been thrilling to see her again, although it had also been shocking to find her so changed. She could have aged ten years. I thought back to Selvin's claim that she was forty-five. In the summer I would not have believed him. But now I could see that she was old, as old as my own mother. And why had she come to the Sixth to shop for clothes? She had not even thought to call me, and she knew that I lived around the corner.

Ethan was at home. He stared as I entered. This confused me, until I remembered that I was carrying more than one shopping bag for possibly the first time in my life.

'What have you been up to?'

I dropped my bags by the dining table. 'Just giving my wardrobe a bit of an overhaul,' I said.

'A bit of an overhaul? It looks as though you've bought up the whole of the Left Bank. What's the occasion? First date?'

'You know I'm not dating.'

'It has to be something. A monk like you doesn't go out shopping for no good reason.'

I was about to explain the assistant's opinion that I could be a model, but I caught myself. Ethan would tease me about it. I went through to the bedroom.

'Aren't you going to give me a demonstration?' he called out.

'Not right now. I'm going to have a bath.'

I needed sanctuary. I liked the bathroom because it was the least dilapidated room in the apartment. The walls were covered in faux-marble tiles and the ceiling was plastered. The other rooms showed the warped wooden beams, and I always found this disconcerting, because it suggested that the whole building could fall down at any moment.

I drew the bath too hot, and it took me a few minutes to adjust to the change in temperature.

Soon my mind filled with possibilities. Élodie had come over from the Eighth for a reason. It could not have been accidental. Élodie never made mistakes. And then I realised that she must have wanted me to run after her. That much should have been obvious. Perhaps it would happen again, and I would have the confidence to seize the opportunity. But did I want to?

I wore one of my new outfits when I emerged from the bathroom. I had tucked a pink silk shirt into a pair of high-waisted trousers, which were held up by a plaited leather belt. The jacket was a deep red lined with satin. Ethan would never have worn it. All of his clothes came from second-hand shops, and he chose them according to what his friends wore.

Ethan was working on a track and I had to tap him on the shoulder.

'What do you think?' I asked as he took his headphones off.

'Man,' he said in amazement. 'You really could have stepped out of the fifties. What were you thinking?'

'I was bored. There's no point in letting my money waste away in a bank account.'

'I don't buy that. You've met someone, haven't you? She likes the whole vintage fashion thing, so you're trying to impress her.'

'Sounds more like something you would do. I don't need to impress anyone. I have better things to do.'

'What, like searching for the meaning of life? At least you're dressed for it now. Add a pipe and a tweed jacket and you'll be a theorist in no time.'

I went to change back into my old clothes.

'By the way,' he called from the other room, 'you're coming to my gig tomorrow night. Café Molotov, eight o'clock.'

'Sorry,' I said. 'I have work to do.'

'Come on, you always say that. It will be good times. I'll introduce you to Marguerite.' He stuck his head around the door. 'You're coming. I'm worried about you, man. You need to cut loose.'

'All right,' I said. 'So long as it doesn't go on too long.'

'Something's definitely wrong with you,' Ethan continued. 'Is it about Sophie?'

'No, of course not.'

'Let me guess: she thinks you're going nowhere, and she wants you to come home.'

'Maybe she does. I don't know. How can you tell?'

'Oh, I can tell. But who cares? You're here, man, in Paris. You've got to live it. She can wait. You should stop taking it so seriously. There are more important things. Like coming to this gig. You might meet the girl of your dreams. And, who knows? She might like your vintage clothes.'

'If you say so.'

'You know, you haven't even told me what happened in Madrid.'

'Because nothing happened in Madrid. You can ask me that sort of thing later, once I've had a drink.'

Ethan found this amusing, and I realised that it was

one of Élodie's lines. I even sounded like her when I said it. He left me to myself, and I returned the new clothes to their rightful place at the bottom of my armoire. There was no use in pretending. They did not suit me.

13

The winter mornings were the best. The Luxembourg
Gardens were empty and the trees were bare. Over the next
week, I took to wrapping myself in as many scarves and
jerseys as I could find, and reading a book down by the
shady Medici Fountain with a coffee in a paper cup. It was
bitter, but it was peaceful. Nobody walked past for hours.
Then, before the spectre of Élodie could begin to haunt
me, I would return to the apartment. Ethan would ask
where I had been, and I would refuse to tell him. Instead I
would ask him about his mad life and his music, because
he was always happy to talk about them, and he always
had something to say that would distract me.

Distraction helped. Study worked most of the time.
Élodie began to fade away, returning in short bursts
whenever I studied Manet. I could see her face in *Olympia*
if I focussed on the shape of her jaw, and her penetrating

stare. She was more familiar here than she was in Titian's voluptuous *Venus of Urbino*, with her enticing, sublime form and her soft breasts. But both paintings were alluring.

I returned to the apartment after a walk one particularly cold evening. Ethan was out, and it was dark and unwelcoming. I drew the curtains and turned the heating up. There was a pot of lentil and potato soup from a few days prior sitting on the stovetop, which I reheated. Ethan had left his bed unfolded once again, and I stuffed the sheets together and folded it into the sofa. I collected up the dirty clothes that he had left on the floor and closed them back into his suitcase, leaving it upright and latched. He would never have cleaned them up, although this was not due to laziness. He had more interesting things to occupy himself with. I did not.

The telephone rang as I was about to ladle the soup into a bowl with a slice of dry baguette. It had to be Sophie.

'Hello?' I said.

'Lawrence, darling.'

I stood with my mouth half-open. After months of expecting to hear her voice, I found myself caught off guard.

'Élodie,' I said. 'What do you want?'

'I want to see you, of course. It has been *far* too long.'

She said this as though it was my fault.

'It has. Why didn't you call me?'

'My life has been rather chaotic. We need to do

something, though. I haven't shown you around Paris. Meet me tomorrow at Clemenceau, by the Grand Palais, ten o'clock. We can have some more fun.'

'What? No, I have university tomorrow. I have a life.'

'University is not a life, Lawrence. Meet me tomorrow. We both know that you want to.'

As I was about to reply she hung up. I held the receiver at arm's length. For once I knew what I wanted. It was satisfying to think that she would wait for me in front of the Grand Palais, possibly for hours, and that she would be humiliated for the first time in her life. She deserved no less.

With a surprisingly clear head I returned to my soup. At that moment I was proud of myself for not succumbing to her allure, and this time it would be for good. I gave the matter no more thought. I was happy with my resolve. And to prove it to myself, I called Sophie.

'Lawrence,' she said. She sounded tired. 'You've forgotten about the time difference again, haven't you?'

'Oh. Sorry. It must be early.'

'It is. Don't worry, I had to get up anyway.'

'So how are you?'

'I'm fine. How about you? What are you writing on?'

'Manet. In fact, I was going to ask you about that. I need to write an analysis of one of his paintings, and I can't decide between *Olympia* and *Argenteuil*.'

'Which one is *Argenteuil*?'

'The one with the couple on the seaside. You know, she's holding these crushed flowers and the boatman is talking to her. Anyway, it's different from *Olympia*. The brushstrokes are more impressionistic. Could be an interesting comparison.'

'Hang on. Let me look it up.'

I heard the tap of her fingers on the keyboard, and then I heard nothing but breathing while I waited for her to say something.

'What do you think?' I said.

'It's not a very nice picture.'

'Don't you think? The paint application is impressive, isn't it? I like that their eyes are indistinguishable.'

'Write about *Argenteuil*, then, if you like it so much. *Olympia* is crude. And everybody has said everything there is to say about it.'

'But *Olympia* is a more beautiful painting, isn't it?'

'No, not really. She's a prostitute. Do you find her attractive?'

'It's not really about her.'

'No. But Lawrence, it doesn't matter what I think of them. You write on whichever one interests you more. Whichever one you have more to say about.'

The next morning I woke earlier than usual. My sleep had been disturbed by some strange and shapeless dreams. Élodie had been the one recognisable figure, drifting in and out of my subconscious like an incessant wave. It felt like something of a failure on my part.

I took a long shower, waiting for my thoughts to loosen and clarify. The hot water ran out. I returned to bed in an effort to keep out the chill, and lay awake for at least an hour. Four floors below, the street sweepers were already at work.

I wanted to see Élodie again. I wanted to be the centre of her attention, and to be on the receiving end of her boundless energy, no matter how misplaced or disturbing it was. But she would have won if I gave in to such desires.

Ethan had made it home, miraculously enough, and he was snoring in the next room. His suitcase had exploded again, his shirts hanging off my reading chair.

When I could bear it no longer I tried on my new clothes. This felt innocent enough. I imagined what would impress Élodie the most, in the alternate reality where I did go to meet her. It was definitely an alternate reality. I struck a pose in the mirror wearing the high-waisted trousers and the pink silk shirt, holding an imaginary martini glass. I had never owned a pink silk shirt before. I drew back and laughed at myself. But I didn't take the clothes off. I sat down on the end of my bed in my sad little apartment. Perhaps this was all my life would ever amount to.

I began to write the essay on Manet, stopping and starting several times. The paintings were next to each other on my computer screen, and I examined them closely. There was unhappiness in *Argenteuil*, while there was loneliness in *Olympia*. But I did not want to write on either of them. I wanted to go and see Élodie.

After two hours I abandoned the essay altogether. Ethan had not yet woken. I took overcoat and gloves and closed the door on him. It was cold out on the street. I was in a trance. But I didn't have to think; I had to walk down to the métro station, from where I only had to purchase a ticket and get on a train.

The train rocked on its loose steel wheels, unsteady beneath my feet. I arrived at Clemenceau ten minutes early. People were milling around the Grand Palais, all moving in different directions as though they were in a Caillebotte painting. I could see down the Champs-Élysées, where a team of construction workers was beginning to put up the Christmas stalls. There was an industrious quality to it all. I thought of the lecture that I was missing, and this heightened my sense of exhilaration. I waited by the steps of the Grand Palais, each minute wound tighter than the last.

Half an hour later I was prepared to abandon all hope. She had played another cheap trick on me. Perhaps she was watching me from around the corner, bent double with hilarity. Or perhaps she was inside the Grand Palais. I wanted to see her gleeful face in the window.

As I was about to return to the métro, I saw her emerge from the crowds on the Champs-Élysées. She glided across the pavement. I had never seen anything like it before. While other women aspired to this swan-like elegance, she made it the simplest act in the world. She was dressed in a black fur coat that was not too ostentatious and fitted tight across her chest. Still she wore the butterfly sunglasses, despite the bleak weather, and still her skin was pale and ghostly. I recognised her handbag, and the perfume. Her scent was so intoxicating that I could smell it before she had drawn up to me. I was taller than her, yet her prevailing force washed over me, and I might as well have slumped to the ground and lain there.

'I thought you might come,' she said. Her eyes were hidden behind the glasses, but it felt as though she was sizing me up again. 'You are different. More robust.'

'You must be imagining it,' I said. The cold accentuated my nerves. She showed her teeth as she smiled. One of them had chipped since I saw her last.

'But the clothes won't do. I hope nobody has said that they suit you.'

'I thought you might have approved.'

'They are an improvement, but not by much. We can do better. Now, come with me, silly boy. We absolutely must catch up.'

I struggled to keep up with her as she headed in the

direction of the twin Arches. She smoked a cigarette as she walked.

'How are you, Lawrence?' she asked. 'Been enjoying yourself, I hope?'

'Not particularly. Frankly, I've been chewed up ever since you abandoned me that night in Biarritz. I thought that you'd never call.' I had rehearsed this response, and it sounded as though I was delivering it on a stage.

'Oh, that.' She said this as though it was a trivial detail in her recollection. 'Don't take it personally. I wanted to see Ed again.'

'So why didn't you come back to the suite?'

'Because he took me out gambling. We had an awfully good time. You missed out. And then I could not go to bed. The night went on.' She must have seen how crestfallen I was. 'Oh dear. You thought that I had abandoned you for good.'

'You didn't call me for three months. What was I meant to think?'

'You should have approached it logically. An erudite boy like you should have found that easy. I have been too caught up in this mad little world to give you the slightest thought. I don't make any apologies on that score.'

'I really did think you had changed for a moment there,' I said. 'What have you been doing that is so much more important than me?'

We walked on in silence. She drew in her chest, and we stopped at a pedestrian crossing while a string of aquamarine buses crossed the avenue. Their exhausts sent up a pall of frosty smoke.

'Let's get a coffee,' she said finally. 'I can't promise any scandalous details, but I can give you the gist of it.'

I followed her across the avenue and down a side street. The crowds thinned and the chain stores disappeared. The café was pressed between two other buildings and would only have been noticed by those who knew where it was.

Élodie continued to smoke, and she ordered two espressos before I could ask for a *café au lait*. I went through the list of things that I had intended to ask her about, the most important being why she had ignored me at the clothes shop. The blind optimist in me thought that perhaps she was about to reveal something. I sat forward, and this annoyed her.

'Do sit back, Lawrence. It makes me uncomfortable.'

I obeyed, sufficiently humiliated. When my coffee arrived I added three cubes of sugar.

'So are you going to tell me a story?' I asked.

'Not until you tell me what you have been up to, young man,' she said. 'You have the look of one who has committed a terrible sin. Confess.'

'You are the only sin that I've ever committed. My

life has been completely free of theatrics ever since our encounter.'

'I find that hard to believe. How is the little lady? Is she still your *lover*?'

'She might be. How's the husband? Is he still your benefactor?'

Élodie drew on her cigarette, pressing it hard between her fingers.

'Now I won't tell you anything.'

I hung my head. 'I'm sorry,' I said. 'That was unfair.'

'You take these things the wrong way, Lawrence.'

'Maybe I do.'

'Yes, well. I asked about the girl. What is there to tell?'

'Nothing much. We talk as often as we can.'

'She doesn't know about me, does she?'

'No.'

'Why not? Are you too crippled by emotional guilt?'

I had not felt as guilty as I thought I would. I drank my coffee absent-mindedly, forgetting that it was hot, and burnt my tongue.

'You could put it that way,' I said. 'I hardly need to ask whether you've told anyone.'

'Oh, it's a wonderful story. I tell it all the time at parties. In fact, I have some people who are dying to meet you this evening. If you can spare the time from your busy schedule.'

'Will Ed Selvin be there?'

'Good Lord, no. I haven't seen that man since Biarritz. I have no idea where he has gone.'

'Really? I was under the impression that you had run off with him.'

'What makes you think that?'

'I saw his wife the next day, alone in the lobby. I inferred that he had left her there.'

'You should never infer anything, Lawrence.'

I was prepared to argue the point, but she put her cup down and prepared to leave. This immediacy was disorienting. Once again I was a seasick passenger on her fast-moving pleasure yacht. I followed her, and left a few coins on the tabletop because she had forgotten to.

'Where are we going?' I asked.

'I am going to show you my Paris. You will enjoy it, I promise.'

'I'll hold you to that.'

Her unstoppable momentum had returned, and I felt myself pulled along. I was not so reluctant this time.

14

We returned to the Elysian Fields. The stream of human traffic was surging, and the noise made it difficult to hold a conversation. Élodie moved so impossibly fast that I could not match her pace.

'You look good, Lawrence,' she said. 'But you neglected one detail. Possibly the most important of them all.'

Before I could ask what that detail might be, she had approached the entrance to a nondescript boutique hidden beneath red awnings and potted shrubbery. The windows showed perfume bottles, which I could easily have mistaken for a gallery display. They were up against a piece of mirrored glass, which made them appear to stretch into infinity.

'Are you suggesting what I think you are?' I said as she was about to enter the shop.

'You need to know the value of masking every detail,'

she said, not choosing her words very carefully. 'Only then can you accompany me to a soirée.'

Stepping into the store, I was greeted by my old enemy: gold. It was in abundance. The fixtures gave off such a sheen that my vision dulled. Everything was reflected in glass and mirrors. Élodie bypassed the women's department, hesitating on a limited edition bottle of *eau de parfum*. I glanced at the price tag. It cost five hundred euros.

The men's department was smaller and less extravagant. I browsed through the fragrances on display, pretending that I knew the differences between them.

'You have to try them first,' Élodie whispered. 'Otherwise you will never make the right choice.'

She picked up a cardboard stick and sprayed one of the testers onto it. I drew it to my nose. Unlike most colognes, it was light and fresh. I liked it, but tried to give the impression that I was thinking it over.

'It's all right,' I said.

'Ah. You have learnt. Try the vetiver. It is more your type.'

I picked out a fresh stick and carefully sprayed from the vetiver bottle. It was a richer bouquet. I could feel it rising up my nostrils, and it hung there for a long time.

'That's the one,' I said.

'Good. It is important to know which scent belongs to you.'

I was going to pay for it, but she cut me off. It was not a platinum card this time, but a gold American Express. The name was different, too, but she handled it so swiftly that I was unable to read it. The odours in the shop were overpowering, and it was a relief to make it out to the street, where the air was thin and permeated by stale cigarette smoke and sewage.

'How did you know that it would suit me?' I asked.

'It is one of my talents. I also know that salmon pink is not your colour. We need to find you a new shirt.'

'Oh. The shop assistant said it suited me better than anybody else.'

'He wanted to sell it,' she said, as though I was the simplest being she had ever come across.

I thought back to the assistant and his insistence that everything looked perfect on me. Perhaps business really had been slow. I didn't dare tell Élodie that in the same shop I had been told that I should become a model.

'Why did you blank me in the clothes shop?' I asked.

'Oh yes,' she murmured. 'I was in a hurry. But it was seeing you that prompted me to call you, darling. You know, I can't stop and talk to every one of my acquaintances. There aren't enough hours in the day.'

'Is that all I am? An acquaintance?'

'Rather.'

I should have returned to the métro station. The insult

was enough to make me falter. But sheer instinct got the better of me. She had selected that perfume for me. She knew me. And now I wanted to know what sort of a shirt she would choose for me.

'So what is this party tonight?' I asked, trying to sound like I didn't care.

'A collection of acquaintances, really. Much like you. They come from all over the place. A few work in fashion, some in film. Possibly a few vagrants will show up, too. You will fit in swimmingly.'

'Thanks a lot.'

'My pleasure. But first we need to get you a shirt.'

We turned off the avenue in the direction of the Rue du Faubourg Saint-Honoré. I had never been to this part of the city before. It was all couturiers and shops with antique fur coats in the windows. The boutiques were inconspicuous and exclusive. It was also confined. I had been trapped in the city since August, and everything about this quartier reminded me how overbearing Paris could be. It was a hectic Pissarro street scene, all grey and brown with hurried brushstrokes.

'So this is the part where you take me to a classy clothes shop that nobody else has heard of?' I said.

'You could say that. This is not an ordinary clothes shop.'

We passed the Élysée Palace and continued towards

the Madeleine. It was hard to stop myself from looking into every one of the shops, all of which were filled with elaborate displays. One gallery specialised in expensive art supplies. Milled paper was stacked on the shelves, and a display of gilded watercolour sets occupied the main window.

'What are you doing, wasting your time with that?' Élodie demanded. 'Do you think that you are a painter because you study art history?'

'I never said that. It is possible to have an appreciation for these things, even if I can't do anything with them.'

'But you can do something with anything. Even clothes, provided they are just the right sort. And this is where Monsieur Bertrand comes in.'

She pointed across the street to another nondescript building. The legend, *Bertrand*, was engraved over the doorway. Ready-to-wear items occupied the main room of the store. Ties, jackets, waistcoats, and paisley silk scarves and cravats. I could see a more enchantingly mechanical world beyond an archway and up a set of steps. A pattern was laid out across the table, surrounded by tape measures and items of machinery that I had never come across before.

The tailor himself—I presumed that this was Bertrand, because he was never introduced—recognised Élodie immediately, and he let out a cry of joy. They kissed on each cheek. Bertrand was a decrepit man with wispy white hair, stooped and wearing a surprisingly casual shirt and gilet. He had oversized spectacles and his skin was like loose leather upholstery. He gave off the scent of cigarettes and dry-cleaned fabric.

'My dear demoiselle Lavelle,' he said, his voice matching the cigarettes. 'Is Monsieur Marcel in need of a new dinner jacket?'

'Why no,' Élodie said. She was flirtatious with Bertrand, even though he was a specimen of gnarled old age. 'In fact, I was hoping that you could do something for this young man. He needs a more becoming shirt for an important social gathering.'

Bertrand must have seen me as an impossible task. I was all too conscious of my bad haircut. There was a mirror by the wall, and I could see that one particular strand was sticking up at the back. I did my best to smooth it down without Bertrand noticing.

'You want only a shirt?' he said pointedly to Élodie.

'It needs to be done for this evening.'

Bertrand held up his arms. 'Impossible. Two days, yes, I can do. But this evening I cannot. I have too many orders to go through today.'

'Oh, Bertrand, really? You used to achieve the impossible for me. Why, I have seen you create masterworks in under an hour.' She moved in closer to him. 'I am certainly prepared to make it worth your while.'

His arms were folded, but it was clear that Bertrand

was going to give Élodie what she wanted.

'How much are you offering?' he said gruffly.

'As much as it takes. Name your price, dear man.'

'Very well, then. But I will not have it ready until at least four o'clock.'

'Perfect. Lawrence—Monsieur Bertrand will take your measurements.'

The measuring process took a long time, and it was difficult to stand still. I could tell that Élodie was watching from beyond the archway, and she could see my abdomen, slender and pale as it was. Was she admiring it? My chest hair had grown a little since the summer, and it made me appear older than I felt. When Bertrand had finished, he excused me with a smile that showed his decaying teeth.

'Does the gentleman perhaps need a ready-to-wear jacket in the meantime?' He directed this question at Élodie rather than me.

'I will see your collection,' I said, before she could answer for me. My French had never sounded so confident before. 'And I will make my decision accordingly.'

'Your boy, he does show some hubris,' Bertrand said to Élodie. It took me a while to realise that Bertrand must have mistaken me for her son.

We browsed through his jackets, which were conventional fare. I wondered if the shirt would be a little more bespoke. Bertrand left for his workshop, and I tried to express these thoughts to Élodie.

'You have to understand the value of tailoring,' she said. 'I cannot believe the number of men who go through life without a tailored suit. It does make a terrible impression.'

'Like Ed Selvin?'

'What about Ed?'

'He didn't wear a tailored suit.'

'Oh. No, he wouldn't. Darling, why do you keep bringing Ed up? He has nothing to do with me. He's a friend from a different world.'

'So you have no feelings for him at all.'

'Maybe. But how do you know I'm not lying?'

'Tell me a lie, then.'

'All right. I love him more than anybody in the world. How was that? Worthy of your approval?'

Was she being serious? I made an effort to pay her no attention, because it upset me to hear her talk that way. One of the jackets was in my size. It had a strip of shiny velvet running around the lapel hem, and cream lining in the arms. Bertrand came out of his workshop to show us that he had already started to cut the pattern.

'It does help to have friends in the right places,' Élodie said, when we were alone on the street. 'You know, I would never have guessed, the day I met that man, that one day he could be so useful to me.'

'Is that how you see people?' I asked. 'Useful devices?'

'Really, Lawrence. Your attempts at psychoanalysis are not as endearing as you might think.'

'Ha. I must be right, then.'

We walked down to the Place de la Madeleine, which was alive with traffic, cars and mopeds careering in every direction. Élodie stopped at the pedestrian crossing.

'Lawrence, darling,' she said. 'I am doing this for your benefit, you know. I am in no mood for disagreement. I just want us to have some fun.'

'You never change, do you?'

Rather than replying, Élodie continued across the road. She stepped in front of the traffic without looking. I followed with more caution. Parisian traffic inspired me with terror. The drivers accelerated once a pedestrian had already stepped out, as though it were all some elaborate trap.

'I need another coffee,' she said. 'And then we are going to buy wine and food for this evening.'

'Oh. Are you hosting the party?'

'I am. Does that surprise you?'

'No, not at all.' This was the truth. I could never have imagined Élodie going to someone else's party. She assumed the role of a host so naturally and yet I thought of her more as a virus.

We stopped at another café, which was as quiet and

formal as the first. I suggested that the cafés weren't as good on this side of the river.

'It depends on what you want from a café,' she said. 'We must go to the Fumoir for lunch. That will dispel any such mythology, I hope. Where do you go in the Sixth?'

I rolled off a few names, and she scoffed at each one.

'Oh yes, you definitely are a student. Danton. I was dragged there once by some American girl who thought it was all the rage. It is one of those places that strives for authenticity, no?'

'You could say that.'

'Yes. What a café sells to the tourists will always be falsified. Even authenticity. And what you end up with is a bad coffee and too many earnest Americans.'

'I thought that you liked Americans.'

'I like them well enough on their own turf. Away from home, they become unbearable. Like children who cannot understand why everything is so different.'

'What a gross generalisation.'

'They are often the most accurate.'

The waiter came by, and this time I ordered two espressos before Élodie could open her mouth.

'My word,' Élodie said. 'You really have learnt something. I should give you a reward for asserting yourself.'

This made me squirm. I sat up straight. We were on the

terrace, despite the chilly weather, which made me grateful for my gloves. Élodie wore neither gloves nor a scarf.

'I forgot to ask,' she said. 'Have you travelled at all since our little escapade in Biarritz?'

These words made me remember, all over again, how we had made love in Biarritz. In this new setting, Élodie was attractive in a different way. Her body was not so flattered in this thick fur coat as it had been in the white leopard-print dress. I could see the hint of her breasts as she leant up against the table, and yet it was this teasing suggestion that made me want to remove her coat. She might have been wearing nothing beneath it.

And then I thought of Sophie, and again I was confronted with the fact that we should have made love in Madrid. But we had not, and it was pointless to dwell on it. I could have told Sophie about Élodie, but I had not. And why had I not travelled since August? The whole point of coming to Europe was to travel, to see the capital cities with their rich histories and their famous artworks and architecture.

'Not at all,' I said. 'I should.'

'I think that you should go to New York. You would like it there. I do not see Paris as a healthy place to spend a long time in, especially at your age. Everything is so cloistered and formal. You go to New York, and I swear to God that you will loosen up within two days.'

'I'll never loosen up. Didn't you say that? I'm a hopeless cause.'

'Perhaps that was a touch cruel. You are improving. Slowly.'

'But can changing location change personality?'

'Are you mad? Of course it can. The surrounding culture affects one's state of mind. That is why I nearly lost my mind in Los Angeles.'

'Nearly?'

Élodie tossed her napkin across the table at me. 'Don't be so mean, Lawrence,' she said. 'It does not suit you.'

'I thought that you wanted me to be mean.'

'Maybe I do. Who could say what I want?'

The coffees were delivered, and I drank mine fast to ward off the cold while Élodie lit up another cigarette. Across the road tourists were milling around the steps of the Madeleine. It was hard to see the attraction of such a grandiose temple, with its unimaginative Corinthian columns rising high, saying everything but meaning nothing. There was honesty in the cracked and soot-stained masonry of Saint-Sulpice, while the Madeleine was impeccable. It was the one church in Paris that managed to look both excessive and rigid.

'It is going to snow,' Élodie said. 'You know, I think it gets earlier each year. It never used to snow until January.'

As the words left her mouth, a fleck blew into my face,

and then another. They came in from the west, and I felt them melting on my cheeks, which were turning red, and I could not help but smile. Élodie smiled too, but not in the usual, posing way. I wished she had taken the sunglasses off. Then I might have known if she was happy.

15

We walked down to the river. The snow was beginning to thicken as we approached the Place de la Concorde, and by the time we had reached the bridge it was falling in a shower. The flakes settled on the mansard roofs and obscured all the cracks and the fallen leaves. We were the only people on the footpath, except for a few who were hurrying for cover.

'I've never seen snow before,' I said. We had stopped in the middle of the bridge. To the east the skyline of monuments was being engulfed by a white cloud. A riverboat slid into sight from the fog downstream. Élodie's breath was frosty, and I felt its warmth as the mist drifted between us. Snowflakes had dotted over her black coat to create a new pattern.

'If this were one of my films,' she said, 'then we would kiss right now.'

She was close to me, and I felt my mouth hang open in anticipation. She laughed at me.

'You should see your face right now,' she said. 'You thought I was being serious, didn't you?'

'No, no I didn't.'

And yet I wanted nothing more than to kiss her. That would have been too perfect, though. It would not have been real.

'This way,' Élodie said. 'We will catch our death out here. I need a drink.'

We hurried across the bridge. My shoes were soaked through. Their smooth soles became skates on the icy pavement. I did my best to keep up without slipping over, wondering how Élodie managed in her high heels.

The first bar that we came across was on the Boulevard Saint-Germain. It was crowded and had the stale smell of wet clothing. Élodie pushed her way to the front of the bar and asked for two coffees with Calvados on the side.

'Interesting idea,' I said.

'Yes. My father used to have it on cold days.'

I stared at her, but Élodie realised her mistake.

'Well, our plans have rather changed,' she went on before I could pry. 'We should drop in on your house of squalor while we are on this side of the river.'

'That's not a good idea. It really *is* a house of squalor right now.'

'I always had you down as the fastidious type, Lawrence. For some reason.'

'It's not me. It's my flatmate, Ethan.'

'Ah, the flatmate. How is he?'

'He doesn't do anything except record his music and think about girls. Everything comes to him so easily. He sleeps all day and drinks all night.'

I said this bitterly, though I hadn't meant to. I wanted to support Ethan and his ambitions, but it was difficult when he had such prospects and I had none of his talent. Not that I envied him. Or perhaps I did. I told myself not to be envious, and to admire him for what he had.

Élodie did not give her rare look of sympathy.

'I know what you're thinking,' I said. 'I should learn from him, have more fun.'

'Not necessarily. You describe him as something of a Neanderthal. You may be many things, but you are not uncouth.'

'Thanks. That's almost reassuring. But I didn't mean to say that I don't like him. We're good friends. We get on.'

'And how was I to know that? You have to be careful about how you describe people, Lawrence. It is easy to cast the wrong impression.'

I drank the Calvados before I drank the espresso. It was a shade sweeter than brandy, and it had a clean, medicinal taste. It offset the bitterness of the coffee well.

'In any case, I want to see the house,' she said. 'Even if I laugh at it. I could do with a laugh.'

'You are unbelievable.'

'Are you prepared to deny it? I can see the place already. Dirty dishes and hair in the sink, onion soup from five weeks ago sitting on the stovetop, and yet you both ask, where is that smell coming from? Your furniture is falling apart, and none of the lights work, but you cannot afford to buy new bulbs, so you sit in the dark.'

This was a surprisingly accurate description, but I pretended that it was not.

'This is based on your experience of student flats, is it?'

'Not at all. I know what you are trying to do there, Lawrence. You will have to wait until I have had a glass of wine before you ask a silly question like that again.'

The snow appeared as a sheet against the window. We had time for another drink. Before Élodie could finish her coffee, I called the barman over and asked for two glasses of the house red, and paid for them.

'Now, is that sufficient leverage for you to tell me the truth?' I asked, once the wine had been poured. 'In all honesty, why did you wait until yesterday to contact me? And don't tell me that you mislaid my number, or anything like that.'

'Darling, please don't do that. Is it so hard to believe that I just felt a compulsion to see you one day?'

'It is when you put it like that.'

'But I have already told you. It's this party. I want to introduce you around.'

'So you never thought about how I might have felt, after you ignored me for months?'

'I haven't ignored you. You are not central to my life. You are a distraction. Not in a bad way, but a distraction nonetheless.'

A distraction? Was this how I saw Sophie? I did not want to be her Sophie. But nor did I believe Élodie. The explanation felt like a cover for something less savoury. The threads of Élodie strung through my memory were all thin and loose, intersecting at odd points and ultimately not making any sense.

'In that case,' I said, 'why are you so generous to me? Are you having a midlife crisis?'

Élodie was touching at her neck again, with those pearly white hands, and I could see the veins standing out on her wrist.

'I keep forgetting that you don't understand these things,' she said. 'Take it for what it is. Nobody will ever be this generous to you again. Think of it that way. And don't use terms that you have heard in films to describe me.'

I folded my arms on the zinc bar top. 'Have I offended you?'

'Nobody can offend me.'

There was no hint of doubt in her voice. But Élodie was becoming progressively unhappy. She took out another cigarette and smoked it, ignoring the sign on the wall that announced a new anti-smoking law. Nobody stopped her. Nobody would dare to stop Élodie from doing as she pleased.

'Do you need to buy some champagne for the party?' I asked after a while.

'Yes. Why do you ask?'

'There is a speciality shop on Saint-Sulpice, around the corner from the apartment. You might like it.'

'Wait a second. I never thought this would happen. You know of an interesting shop that I have never heard of. An impressive achievement on both fronts, Lawrence. Did you take my advice to heart?'

'You didn't give me any advice. I felt the need to celebrate my birthday with something, and that was it.'

'Your twenty-first?' she said, cheering up. 'I hope that you had someone to celebrate it with.'

'Only my flatmate. And he had a show that night, so I had to go along to that, and had a thoroughly bad time.'

'Wonderful. It gets better. Tell me more.'

'There isn't much more to tell, trust me. I made myself three Kir Royals for lunch and lost myself for the rest of the day.'

'Now that must be a joke.'

'It's true. But I don't see why people make such a big deal out of it. There's nothing special about that birthday. It's an arbitrary number.'

'It is an arbitrary number you will never identify with again. You need to learn to make things like that last, Lawrence. You can relive them forever. And that really is incorrigible behaviour. When was your birthday?'

'Last month.'

'Then it is not too late. We can celebrate it this evening.'

'No, really. It's not necessary.'

'I will be the judge of that, thank you very much. I insist on it. We must at least have a toast. And, who knows? I might give you a belated present.'

This attracted my attention.

'Sure,' I said, as casually as I could. 'Whatever you see fit.'

'On one condition, though.'

'Yes, I thought there might be a catch.'

'Be charming tonight. It will make the whole thing so much more bearable.'

'Right. No pressure at all, then.'

'Now really, Lawrence, I won't hear you say such a thing. You can do it. Act naturally.'

She drained her wine glass. The wine matched her lipstick as the two touched. The snow had abated, although the clouds remained low and grey.

'Come on,' she said, 'let's go.'

Out on the boulevard snowflakes hung in the trees, but otherwise the snow had not settled. I shivered. No amount of clothing could block out this chill. Élodie continued to talk as we walked, explaining that she disliked this end of Saint-Germain-des-Prés, and that the area around the intersection with Rue Bonaparte was a far better place to shop.

'Anything within the triangle formed by Raspail and the Rue de Rennes is fine,' she said. 'Have you been to the Bon-Marché? Well, no, it is not your sort of place. It is flypaper for rich women.'

'Including you?'

'If I have nothing better to do. But where do you go? There must be some filthy student shops over in the Fifth that you frequent.'

'I shop for bargains. I have to.'

'Then you will enjoy the sale day in January. Although you will have to fight tooth and nail with the other bargain hunters.'

I half listened. Her advice served no purpose, when I had no desire to waste money on those luxury goods that returned nothing apart from fleeting satisfaction. But that was not true of Élodie. She could make the satisfaction last a lifetime. Could I ever experience the same thrill from shopping, rather than the confusion and guilt?

We passed the Romanesque covered market, and Élodie insisted on purchasing foie gras and Italian hams. I had never been to this market, even though it was around the corner from my apartment, because it was too expensive. The same could be said for the bakery on the Rue de Seine, where Élodie bought a paper bag of four baguettes. She gave these to me, naturally enough.

'You really have the finest situation here, Lawrence,' she said in a rare show of genuine excitement as we left the bakery. We pushed past an American couple who were blocking the doorway, fascinated by the window display of stylised *bûches de Noël*, with their spider webs of cream and chocolate at either end. 'I am envious. One of the best markets in Paris, one of the best bakeries, and neither of them more than a few steps away. Oh, and look.'

She stopped at the chocolatier's frontage. Three lighted pillars in the window supported boxes of macarons, in varying colours and styles.

'We absolutely must,' Élodie said.

The chocolatier insisted on showing us the full range of macarons, and he chatted with Élodie about how they were made and that he used green tea powder imported all the way from Japan. We stopped by the champagne boutique on Saint-Sulpice, where the shopkeeper suggested one of the most expensive cuvées. I was expecting Élodie to rebuke him for this lapse in etiquette, but she bought several bottles of it. I could not keep up with the weight of these new purchases, and by the time we had carried them to the fourth-floor apartment, my arms were begging for release. Élodie was enjoying it.

'Your building has a rustic feel,' she said as we reached the top of the staircase. 'Have you noticed that the landings slope?'

She slipped off her sunglasses. She had deep lines under her eyes, the sort that no amount of make-up could ever hide. They had not been there in Biarritz.

'Why do you wear those in the middle of winter?' I asked.

'Because nobody else does, of course.'

The door took a long time to open, with its rickety upper and lower latches, and when it did I would have been happy to close it again. Ethan was absent, but his presence lingered in the form of breakfast dishes, his unmade bed and a distinct aroma that hung in the air. Élodie did not disappoint.

'Hell, it really is worse than I thought it would be,' she said happily. It was colder inside the apartment than out, and remnants of snow clung to the windowpanes. I turned the old gas heater on, while Élodie took a cautious step inside.

'Can I get you anything?' I asked.

'No, I don't think so. I might well catch something.

Get that tie I bought you in the summer and we can leave.'

The thin black tie from Biarritz was at the bottom of my armoire. It was badly creased. I tried to straighten it out so Élodie wouldn't be able to tell.

In the main room Élodie was poring over my possessions. She was completing a circuit, stopping at each surface and going through all of the items on them. She paused on a copperplate engraving of a Madonna and Child, which had come with the apartment. It was the only piece of art that I owned, so it had to stay on display, to inspire me.

'That is rude, you know,' I said. She glanced up from a photograph of Sophie and me outside the Prado, which I kept on my writing desk.

'Why put them on display, then?' she asked. 'I like this one. I'm surprised. She is prettier than I thought. But she tries too hard to pose for the camera. Have you seen her since then?'

'No, she is stuck in New Zealand.'

'Poor thing. She must be heartbroken. But consider this, Lawrence: you might as well be free. Why don't you run off somewhere? Have a proper holiday of your own down in Capri or Corfu. Somewhere fabulous.'

'That depends. Would you come with me?'

'I can't go to Capri again, darling. I've done it to death.' She examined the photograph closer. 'This is funny, you know. She is trying too hard, but you could almost be enjoying yourself here.'

Over her shoulder I could see that my hair was too long in the photograph, as it still was, and I had not shaved well that day. But I was happy, happier than I remembered being at any time in Madrid.

'So I don't look like that all the time?'

'No. I see little flashes of it, every now and then. You try to hide them.'

We had come close together. Élodie's lips were not so far away from mine. I hesitated. What did I want? If I kissed her it would prove to her that I could be assertive and take charge, if I so desired. I wrapped my arm around her lower back. But Élodie drew away and replaced the photograph.

'Come along,' she said coolly. 'I am going to show you an alternative to this filth.'

I cursed myself for my stupidity. I was staring out at myself from the photograph, me with my excessive smile and one too many shirt buttons undone. And Sophie was staring out at me too, although she was avoiding the lens. I put the photograph in my desk drawer.

16

I suggested that we take the métro over to the Eighth, but Élodie refused to hear a word of it. Nor would she take a taxi. Instead she led the way down the Rue de Seine, which was a colourful street lined with many galleries and alleyways that led into tree-filled courtyards.

'You must read some more Baudelaire,' she said. 'The point of walking is to see and to be seen. What does one see on the métro?'

'Not much. It is faster, though.'

'Indeed. Time is irrelevant to us.'

One of the galleries was showing a photography exhibition. Élodie caught me by the arm and pulled me over. The work in the window was a black-and-white view of Manhattan. The shadows and exposure were manipulated to give it a surreal quality.

'What's interesting about that?'

'Oh darling, it's beautiful. This man has captured how I feel about New York in one shot.' Her eyes were obscured by the sunglasses, but they must have been fixed on me. 'You must go there, Lawrence. Promise me that you will, one day. If you want to have some real fun.'

There was nothing I could say. Did I want to have real fun? Élodie's interpretation of it was not the same as mine.

The street opened out at the riverbank, which was a relief after the narrow stone lanes of the Sixth. The *bouquinistes* were shut up against the weather, and their ancient green lids were covered with anarchist graffiti. I headed for the Pont des Arts.

'Where are you going?' Élodie called out. 'That bridge is no good. Too many sickening lovers.'

There were tourists on the bridge taking pictures of one another with their mobile phones, but there were also artists selling charcoal portraits and a man with a guitar and unruly dreadlocks. The couples were all enjoying themselves, but whether or not they were in love was another question. Élodie started down the quay towards the Pont du Carrousel.

'How do you know that they are in love?' I asked as I caught up.

'Because they aren't really in love. They attach a padlock to the railing and throw away the key. Blind sentimentality at its very worst.'

'They aren't all like that. You try so hard to be cynical. It doesn't do you justice.'

'Perhaps not. It is who I am, though. The world never ceases to underwhelm me. But you shouldn't think like that. It is a bad example to follow, and it can get you into all sorts of trouble.'

I was going to ask her what sorts of trouble it had got her into, but I stopped myself. I had my own theories on the matter.

'Where is your apartment?' I asked as we crossed the bridge and walked through to the other side of the Place du Carrousel, alongside the Louvre. Tourists stood in an orderly line in front of the Pyramid, which was beckoning them into an overpriced underworld. The old buildings of the Louvre somehow showed none of their age.

'I never said it was my apartment.'

'Oh. Whose is it, then?' I asked.

'It might as well be mine. It is on the Rue Lord Byron. Rather a long way off. Christ, we might have to get a taxi. I cannot walk up there in these shoes.'

'You contradict yourself a lot, don't you?'

'But I am not indecisive. You cannot accuse me of that.'

'Perhaps not. Your problem is that you make too many decisions.'

She stopped walking and leant against a lamppost. I had been through the Place du Carrousel many times on my way to see the paintings in the museum. While it inspired a centuries-old sense of awe, it became less impressive with each visit. The triumphal arch opposite the Pyramid was grandiose, unrestrained in its use of pink marble and gold trimming. It was a neoclassical feast that nobody could finish. The sun was coming out from beyond the fast-burning snow cloud, and this illumination improved the scene. Élodie's sunglasses were no longer ridiculous.

'Oh look,' she said. I followed her gaze towards two people who were coming through the archway that led onto the Rue de Rivoli. 'You will never guess who that is.'

'No, I probably won't.' They were faceless figures from this distance.

Élodie waved, and one of them waved back. 'It's Ed. Would you believe it?'

My whole body tensed. As we drew closer, I saw that it really was Ed Selvin. He was wearing an overcoat and a patterned scarf, neither of which did much to complement his figure. He did not appear affected by the cold, and this must have been due to his extra layer of insulation. My cheeks and nose were pink, while his remained a sickly shade of white. He was with a girl, but she was not Vanessa. She was younger and blonder. Her face was hidden beneath too much blush, and she wore a tweed coat and knee-high boots, between which was a hint of her bare, pale legs.

'Ed, darling, what a coincidence,' Élodie said. 'You remember Lawrence, don't you?'

Selvin took in my new clothes as though I were part of a displeasing museum display. 'Larry,' he said. 'How could I forget you?' He did not introduce his latest piece of jewellery, and like Vanessa she stood removed from the conversation. 'What are the chances of a meeting like this? Say, we should get a drink together.'

'Why not make it lunch?' Élodie said.

'All right.' He directed his attention to the bags we were carrying, and for a moment I thought that he might offer to carry some of mine. This proved to be wishful thinking. 'What's with the bags? Are you in the charitable business?'

'No, darling. I'm having a party tonight; I completely forgot to invite you. Everyone will be there. You must come along. I thought that you would be in New York.'

'I've come over here to do some more talent scouting,' he said. This made me look at the girl a little more carefully. 'Leaving tomorrow. So unfortunately I've already made plans for tonight.'

'That really is too bad,' Élodie said. 'Gosh, it is far too cold to be standing here. Tell me all about your wicked plans before we get to the restaurant.'

We walked towards the Cour Carrée. I had always liked the passage that linked it to the Carrousel. An old man played the cello, practically in the dark, and there was often a congregation around him. There was something communal and reverential about it. He kept his eyes down beneath a cloth hat, and he refused to be photographed. But there was no mystery to him; he was a man bound to his occupation, and nothing else mattered to him. I held back and watched him.

Élodie continued to enthuse. She made herself even more ridiculous around Selvin, and they walked close together. The footpath in this passage was wide enough for three people, so I was left to bring up the rear.

'I hope that we haven't interrupted anything,' she said.

'Not at all. We were going to have a drink right about now. What have you been doing all this time? How's Marcel?'

'You know perfectly well how Marcel is. And I have been doing nothing out of the ordinary. I felt a desire to cut loose today, though. To enjoy ourselves while we still can.'

'And are you enjoying yourself?'

'Ever so much. You can't begin to imagine. Lawrence is being a wet blanket, though.'

This stung. Perhaps Élodie's jocular treatment of me masked something else. Selvin must have seen my blush. I wished that I could have some control over it, and willed the blood to leave my cheeks.

The chosen restaurant was beside the Saint-Germain l'Auxerrois, and it had orange awnings. They were the only injections of colour in this otherwise grey corner of the city. What few trees stood on this street were skeletal, and looked as though they might disintegrate in a gust of wind. There were no free tables in the *salle*. The waiter recognised Selvin, even though I presumed that he did not live in Paris. He might have had a pied-à-terre, a concept that I did not understand. At his request, we were shown to the private room and given a table by the window. The waiter took our shopping bags and coats and pushed our chairs in. We were a motley group. Selvin's attachment was my age, and yet she could never have passed for my sister. Or so I hoped.

'How is New York, darling?' Élodie said to Selvin. 'I should so love to be there right now. This town is too dreary in winter.'

'I couldn't agree more,' Selvin said. His bad posture irritated me. It gave him the appearance of a sleek hog dressed up and made to sit at the table as part of some cruel joke. 'New York stays alive in the wintertime. This place closes up for months. I find it terribly dull.'

'I hope you don't find me terribly dull?'

'No, you light it up.'

'Oh please, you silly man. Do you expect me to swallow such shameless flattery?'

'I do.'

We were the only diners in this part of the restaurant.

Blinds obscured most of the windows. It was designed with privacy in mind. Bookshelves formed the surrounding walls. Although I would usually have disliked this injection of quaintness, it created an atmosphere that Manet could have turned into a smoky drinking den. A shaded lamp hung over the table from the ceiling, skewed at an angle and adorned with tassels.

Their conversation continued to exclude, and I felt myself falling into the same shipwreck site as the nameless girl, who was smiling at nothing. It was Biarritz all over again. But this time I resolved to involve myself in the conversation.

'This is a nice place,' I said to Élodie. 'You've been here before, haven't you?'

'I suggested it, Lawrence, so it would make sense. But I am glad that it stands up to your advanced tastes.'

'Ed, have you been here too?' I said. 'The waiter did recognise you.'

'No,' he said. 'You must have got that wrong.'

'So I take it that you don't come to Paris all that often?'

'Your friend here is rather impertinent,' he said to Élodie, 'isn't he?'

'Yes, he is. Do stop it, Lawrence, you will embarrass yourself.'

'I was wondering,' I said, 'because it's a coincidence. You turning up here, when you live in New York.'

'Lawrence, darling,' Élodie started to say, but Selvin cut across her.

'No matter, Élodie. There's nothing wrong with a bit of innocent curiosity.' He faced me with sunken eyes, which made him look older than he had before. 'I have a branch of my business here, so I have to come over every now and then. I've always had an affinity with French culture, you know. So it's an excellent excuse to be at home here. But you're young. I wouldn't expect you to understand these things.'

'And what is your business?'

'I'm a filmmaker. Did Élodie not tell you that?'

'She did. Although I don't know what sort of films you make.'

'Wow, kid. You couldn't sound much more suspicious. I swear I'm not a criminal, Your Honour.'

'I wasn't accusing you of anything. I thought that I should know something about you before we had lunch together.'

Élodie and the girl were staring at me with some incredulity. Perhaps foolishly I thought of this as an achievement to be proud of. Selvin was speechless for the first time since we had met. I drank some water, keeping my gaze levelled at him.

'How does Lawrence look to you, darling?' Élodie said. She was nervous, close to panic. 'He picked out these clothes on his own, and I am getting my tailor to do him a shirt for this evening.'

'Very nice,' Selvin said. His brow was flat. It gave nothing away. 'Not many people could pull that style off. I can't think of the word to describe it. Retro, perhaps. But that doesn't quite do you justice, does it Larry?'

I didn't know how to react and started to read the menu. My shame must have been palpable. Élodie glanced over at me a few times, and her intimidating expression demanded that I cheer up, or else. This made me feel worse. I gave my order in clumsy French, while Élodie delivered both hers and Selvin's in familiar fashion. The girl was indeed French and she ordered a vegetarian salad, with no wine.

'How are the studies in art history, kid?' Selvin asked when the menus had been cleared and our glasses set. 'Have you figured out what to do with them yet?'

'No,' I said. 'I don't have much of a vocation.'

'Who needs a vocation? The point is, are you enjoying them, or wasting time and money while pretending to enjoy them? There's a difference.'

'I suppose I am enjoying them, yes.'

'You *suppose*. I should have guessed it.'

'I think that any experience is worth it, so long as you learn something about yourself in the process.'

'Oh Lawrence,' Élodie said, as if reprimanding a

schoolboy. 'None of that philosophical nonsense is welcome at this table. Go to your tutorial at the Sorbonne if you want to be taken seriously.'

'Hear, hear,' Selvin said. 'University can't teach you about life. Life itself is the only thing that can. How's that for a philosophy?'

He said this with an exaggerated accent and touched his finger to his chin. I hoped that I didn't look or sound like that when I talked, but I could never be sure.

'Seriously, Larry, why are you wasting your time at that place? From what I hear, the Sorbonne is so outdated they don't even use computers to run the place.'

This was true. My file was kept in a dusty ledger in some attic, handwritten with a fountain pen.

'So what alternative would you propose?' I asked.

'How about *anything*? You could always stop studying like your life depends upon it, and start living a life.'

'I am missing a lecture right now. So it isn't as though my life depends on it.'

'Seriously? You're missing a whole lecture? Larry, all I can suggest is that you quit waiting around at university for something to fall into your lap.'

'I'm not,' I said. 'Things are happening.'

I was sure that this was true. I just didn't know what they were.

17

The lunch was interminable, with neither Élodie nor Selvin wanting it to end. The girl responded to one of Selvin's jokes but otherwise remained silent. The food took forever to arrive, and when it did I had no appetite.

'Lawrence, darling,' Élodie said as I set my cutlery down. 'Whatever is the matter? Are you the same young man who practically wolfed a bouillabaisse in Hendaye?'

'Maybe not.'

'But you are such a twig. I hate to think what you have been eating in your squalid existence. If anything at all.'

'I don't have much choice. I've gone off meat because it is too expensive.'

'How sad. I hope you haven't turned into one of those silly vegetarians.'

This had to be for the girl's benefit.

'Not really,' I said. 'More out of necessity. But I have

to say that none of the food around here does much for anybody. The women eat pastries, and it doesn't change anything.'

'It is called the French Paradox,' Élodie said. 'And I wish it were true. Unfortunately, what it boils down to is that the girls here spend their days finding new and obsessive ways to stay svelte.'

'Do you?'

'Oh, such impertinence. I don't need to. I can go a whole day with nothing but a cup of coffee, if I so desire.'

There was something that I admired about this declaration, though it made Selvin wince. I could remember how Élodie's body had felt under my hands, and my memory was of a defined skeleton with little between the bones. But I also remembered the teardrop shape of her backside, and how our legs had touched together and played beneath the bedsheets. Her body was strong— not malnourished. Our eyes made contact for the briefest second, and it felt as though she was reading my mind.

Selvin took out his pocket humidor once he had finished his meal, and the unfortunate waiter asked him to smoke it outside.

'So this place has a bit of a misnomer?' he said in response. I suspected that, like Élodie, he was unaccustomed to denial. The waiter tried to explain that it was a new legal requirement and that the restaurant could be fined.

Selvin agreed reluctantly and picked up his overcoat.

'I'll come with you,' Élodie said. 'I could do with a cigar.'

I was not invited this time, and I was left with the girl, who was restless. Beneath her coat she wore a little black dress, and around her wrist was a charm bracelet. It was the one detail that made her as young as me.

'Sorry, I didn't catch your name,' I said in French, once the two grown-ups had left.

'My name is Isabelle.' Her voice was delicate and husky.

'Pleasure to meet you, Isabelle. And what do you do?'

'I accompany Monsieur Selvin, if you must know,' she said, affronted. I had forgotten that the French never asked one another what they did—it was considered impolite. 'He has promised to start my acting career.'

I could imagine what such accompaniment would involve. 'How nice,' I said. 'And how much do you know about Monsieur Selvin's work in film?'

'Not much. He has promised to tell me all about it when I come to live in America, though.' She blushed at this. 'My English is not so good. He says he will pay for classes.'

I considered telling her what I knew of Selvin's business, not to mention his romantic history, and insisting that she run while she had the chance.

'How long have you known him for?' I asked.

'A few weeks. We met at an industry party. I wanted to…how do you say?…*Get my foot in the door.*' She said this in English. 'Anyway, I told him that I had always wanted to see America. New York, in particular. Paris is such a dull city these days. Everything happens in America. And he promised to make my dream come true.'

She was so young, and so assured of this mythology, that I couldn't help but pity her. But then I wondered if her actions really were that passive. She might have known what she was doing, and perhaps Selvin was about to get a shock.

Out the window I could see the Place du Louvre, and the end of the old grey palace that tried to be beautiful. It was a desolate scene. The cobblestones were layered with cigarette ends and dead leaves. Élodie and Selvin were smoking their cigars on the corner of the Place. He was bent over her figure, presumably to protect her from the wind. I would never have thought to do something like that.

Watching them through the glass felt like an intrusion. I called the waiter over to order more wine, and asked Isabelle if she was sure that she did not want any.

'It stains my teeth,' she said. 'And Monsieur Selvin wouldn't want me to add to the bill.'

'What do you mean?'

'That I don't want to be in his debt.'

'Is that not a good place to be?'

'No. He doesn't like it. It makes him anxious.'

Was I indebted to him? I tried to remember if he had paid for anything in Biarritz. I was only really indebted to Élodie's husband. If he was still her husband.

'Do you know anything about her?' I asked.

'Who?'

'Élodie. Has he talked of her?'

'Not much. But Monsieur Selvin told me that we might run into her today.'

'Oh. How did he know about that?'

'About what?'

'Élodie didn't know that Ed was in town today.'

Isabelle's expression suggested that I was the thickest man she had ever encountered, and I supposed that this in itself was an achievement.

'Of course she did. She talked to him yesterday.'

Élodie and Selvin were coming inside. Isabelle was sublimely detached from the situation and I wanted to tell her that she was mad to trust such a dishonest man. But I wanted to know more. I was about to ask her what else she knew of Élodie when the waiter came over with my wine. He spent a while pouring it and waited for me to taste it.

'My, that was refreshing,' Élodie said, sitting back at the table. 'You should try an afternoon smoke at least once, Lawrence. It clears the mind.'

Selvin kept his coat on and remained standing. 'We should go somewhere else for a coffee,' he said. 'That's the etiquette here, isn't it?'

'It might as well be,' Élodie said. 'Don't worry, Ed, I will get this.'

It occurred to me that I should do the gentlemanly thing. 'I'll get it,' I said. 'It must be my turn.'

Élodie was incredulous. 'Don't be silly, Lawrence. Save your money to buy new light bulbs, or to hire a cleaning service.'

'No, I'm getting it,' I said with the sort of vehemence that I could not usually keep up. 'I owe you at least this much.'

'Hey, if the kid wants to pay, let him pay,' Selvin said. 'I'm not complaining.'

'All right,' she said. 'If you insist.'

The waiter delivered the bill, which I took without allowing anybody else to see. The sum was substantial, and I questioned my decision. But I gave the waiter my credit card, with what I hoped was the right degree of nonchalance.

'I know a good place for coffee on the Rive Gauche,' I said, continuing to masquerade as a seasoned local. 'Not too far. Unless you had other plans.'

Élodie did, but Selvin cut across before she could protest.

'We're in your hands, Larry,' he said. 'I'm interested to see what you come up with.'

The challenge was set. Although I could tell that Selvin would have a problem with whatever venue I chose, he could not have predicted my encyclopaedic knowledge of cafés in the Sixth. I had made a point of studying them on my endless walks, including the famous ones where Hemingway and Camus may or may not have drunk absinthe. They were not the best cafés. The best ones had opened recently and had no history.

I led the way across the Place du Louvre. From here one could see the spires of both Saint-Sulpice and the Église Saint-Germain, standing alongside the twin monoliths, Montparnasse and Eiffel. These four towers dominated the skyline, separate but strangely unified. Élodie made the same objections to the Pont des Arts as I walked towards it, but this time I forged my own path through the tourists and the street artists. No matter what Élodie thought, I liked this busy bridge more than the other crossings. With such an eclectic mix of people moving over the one set of boards, something was always happening. A spaniel barked and bounded towards us from the other side, its ears flapping in the breeze.

'How can you not like this?' I asked Élodie, once the dog had sniffed our trouser cuffs and returned to its master.

'You will understand why when you have seen more

of the world.' Her face was framed by the postcard view towards the Île de la Cité, and it fitted rather well. 'Don't forget how young you are, Lawrence.'

'I thought that you wanted me to seem older than I really am.'

'You can take these things too far. Nothing ever comes of trying to show off.' She said this in a low voice, so that Selvin would not hear. He was walking at a distance from Isabelle, checking the messages on his phone. Élodie was wearing the same jewellery that she had in Biarritz, except the ring with the strange inscription was missing. Had she and Marcel separated? If that was the case, whose apartment had she been talking about? Perhaps she owned one. What would an apartment of hers be like? I imagined art objects and half-unpacked suitcases and dresses strewn everywhere. She would have an eccentric cellar of wine and grainy old photographs of distant relatives on the walls, with a story for each of them.

The café was on the Carrefour de l'Odéon, near my apartment. I took a table on the terrace, so that we could enjoy the view. I had grown a habit of sitting on this terrace and reading for a whole afternoon. I would make a single coffee last for hours, which annoyed the waiters. This time they were more attentive. They could see Élodie and Selvin's wealth, and they paid more attention to it. I ordered coffee and Calvados. Élodie noticed but said nothing.

'This sure is nice,' Selvin said, folding his hands across his lap. It was an unattractive pose. He might not have been conscious of his mannerisms. He might not have thought about himself in any such detail.

'It is,' I said. 'And you can smoke if you like.'

'You can? They haven't banned smoking outdoors, too?' He produced the humidor and offered me a cigar.

'Come on, Lawrence,' Élodie said. 'I will not stand for this. Have a smoke.'

They had orchestrated things so that it would be rude to refuse. I took the cigar and the cutter, and set about performing the ritual. I got it right this time, and hardly spluttered when the first cloud of smoke billowed into my mouth. I was glad when the coffee arrived to wash the overpowering flavour away.

'That tie of yours is intimidating me,' Selvin said. 'Do you always go around dressed like a prep?'

'It depends on the occasion.'

'Great, so now I feel underdressed.' His own collar was loose.

'Don't listen to him,' Élodie said. 'You look absolutely striking. Ed is jealous because he can't wear a tie these days.'

This made me more self-conscious. It occurred to me that I might look a little odd, and—worst of all—that I might stand out. I took another puff of the cigar. It was bearable this time. The flavour reminded me of Biarritz.

'So what are you doing this evening that is so much more important than my party?' Élodie said. Perhaps the switch in conversation was for my benefit. 'I feel betrayed.'

'I wish I could come to your party. It's a meeting with this French director. I owe him dinner at the Ritz. And this little lady needs to accompany me.' It was his first reference to Isabelle, and it might as well have been her only role in the proceedings.

'How terrifically boring that sounds,' Élodie said. 'I wish that you could duck out of it. We are bound to have a good time, and even more so if you are there to help out.'

'What is it in aid of?'

'Do I need an excuse? I haven't seen these people in ages. And for once I want to be the centre of attention.'

'Fair enough,' he said. 'The next time you're in New York we can have our own party. How about that? And I'll buy the champagne.'

'What a fine deal.'

Selvin checked his watch once he had finished his coffee.

'I'm sorry to abandon you, Élodie,' he said. 'But we must be going. Where are the taxis around here?'

I had been expecting him to stay longer, and it was a relief to think that I would have Élodie to myself again. I directed him to the nearest rank on the boulevard. He shook my hand. 'I'm sure we'll see each other again sometime,' he said. 'And remember what I said—find something to do. There aren't enough years in a lifetime to be studying art history.'

'Do call me, or something,' Élodie said. 'Before you leave tomorrow.'

He kissed her on both cheeks, and then he led Isabelle away by pushing his hand to her back. He waved from the corner. I was not sad to see him go.

18

We stayed on the café terrace while Élodie finished her cigar. The chaotic comings and goings of the Carrefour played out before us. The passing traffic swerved drunkenly away from the boulevard and up the narrow side streets. Paris somehow made beauty out of this chaos. My coffee was murky and cold, but I finished it nonetheless.

'That was a coincidence,' I said, 'seeing Ed like that.'

'It was,' she said. 'I am sorry that you don't like him.'

'He's grown on me a little.'

'You are holding yourself better. But don't take it too far. I don't want you to lose your charm.'

'So you want me to be both charming and assertive. What makes you think I can do that?'

'Just a hunch. Lawrence, I'm afraid I have to ask you about the girlfriend again.'

'She has a name, you know.'

'Yes, *Sophie*. Where are you going with her? What happens when you return to New Zealand? Will you spend the rest of your life with her? Pop out a few children and buy a house in the suburbs? Will she sacrifice her career for your sake? What future can there be in a relationship with somebody so dull?'

'She isn't dull. And people don't have to consign themselves to a future like that anymore. It is possible to be happy without knowing where we're going.'

'But she will want to know, darling. And you will have to tell her something.'

'Perhaps I won't return to New Zealand.'

'Then do something about it. Don't lead her on. I won't let you waste your energy on something that will never happen. You have left it too long to be her first, you know. Fireworks never go off twice.'

She put out the cigar in the ashtray, crushing it into flakes with her fingers, and started to pick up the various shopping bags.

'Let's go, darling, it is getting on. And I will catch a frightful cold if I stay out here any longer.'

I was upset from the talk about Sophie. Nobody had ever told me how to deal with relationships. People only told you to have the relationship in the first place. It was seen as no more than a good thing. Where to from there? The bad inevitably followed the good. It made me sad to think that the holiday in Madrid could have been my happiest time with Sophie, and that from here things would get worse.

The sky had gone pearly, and I hoped that it might snow again. I made sure to pay for the coffees and we ambled around the corner to the boulevard, gliding through the streets while everybody else walked fast. Time no longer mattered. The taxi took us from the Boulevard Saint-Michel across Châtelet and up the Rue de Rivoli. The city looked different from inside a car, but not necessarily better. The architecture was already close enough to a museum display without an added pane of glass.

'This man is cheating us,' Élodie said, bending in so close that I could smell her perfume. 'He is taking the long way, with more traffic, so that we will have to pay more. He must think we are tourists.'

'Trust me, nobody could mistake you for a tourist.'

'Such a cheap thing to say, Lawrence. But I do appreciate it. You look...*transitional* is the word, I think. Somewhere in the middle.'

'Between what and what?'

'Ah, that is the question. Between impoverished student and impoverished fashion model, perhaps.'

'Is that an improvement?'

'*An improvement*. You really are funny, Lawrence. Don't ever change that. I will be disappointed if you become a bore. There are too many of them in the world.'

'So I'm not a bore, but I am a wet blanket.'

'Oh darling. Please never pull that passive-aggressive act on me; it really is off-putting. I said that for Ed's benefit, you know.'

'You say a lot of things for Ed's benefit.'

And she knew it. She bowed her head. I was defeated. I wanted to argue with her. But that would make me the wet blanket again.

Her street was close to the Arc de Triomphe. It was narrow, residential, with no pedestrians. The apartment building was strikingly modern, with Haussmann-style blocks on either side. Its plate-glass windows and clean sandstone were somehow improper.

'This is different,' I said as we trudged through to the lobby, which was tiled with a slippery marble.

'Marcel prefers not to live in any of those old apartments,' she said. She had removed her sunglasses. Her eyes showed none of the glimmer that I remembered, even under such harsh lighting.

'So this is your husband's apartment?'

'Of course it is. But he is no longer my husband.'

'Oh. I'm sorry. Why didn't you tell me?'

'It is hardly your business, Lawrence. In any case, he is out of town right now, so I can do whatever I wish.'

'He's given you permission to live here when he's not around, then?'

'Lawrence, you never cease to amaze me.'

'All right,' I said, after a few false starts. 'So you've taken over your ex-husband's apartment to throw a party. *You* never cease to amaze me, Élodie. Isn't that illegal?'

'If he finds out. But he won't.' She was both casual and defiant, but I could sense that there was something more intense lurking behind this. I felt a strong urge to provoke it out.

'This is wrong on all sorts of levels,' I said.

'Isn't it just? Don't worry. He won't know a thing, and we will have a fabulous time.'

I faced her with my sternest of stares, hoping that she might melt beneath it. She showed no signs of discomfort.

'Why did you divorce him?' I said. 'Did he find out about me?'

She snorted. 'You do flatter yourself.'

'Tell me why. I deserve to know.'

'Please, Lawrence, don't do this to me,' she said in a voice that was somehow both aggressive and childish. 'You don't understand these things. It is unfair to make judgements when you have barely seen a fraction of the evidence. Trust that I know what I am doing, because you most certainly do not. No matter how you see me.'

The elevator stopped on the sixth floor. Élodie walked out. I had the familiar urge to escape. But again I defied it. This time it was out of sheer curiosity that I followed her.

'Why should I trust you?' I asked.

Her hands shook as she tried to find the keys in her handbag. 'Because you know no better. Can you deny it?'

'No.'

'Then trust me.' Her smile was deranged. 'We need to have some real fun. I can't have any fun on my own. Come inside, you silly boy.'

The apartment was not Élodie's. It was austere, lacking personality. The art on the walls had no feeling in its choice, and none of it was compelling. Everything was laid out perfectly, much like a hotel suite. A grand piano stood in the middle of the room, but unlike other pianos I had seen it was not decorated with family photographs or knitted throws. The furniture ran through the hue of glass, metal and suede with minimal patterning. It was all surface and no substance.

'I do like this place,' Élodie said, 'because there is no view of that damned hideous Eiffel Tower. But it still gets enough light.'

Her tone was curiously self-aggrandising, as though she had won some sort of an argument.

'Do you play the piano?' I asked.

'I don't have the time for such nonsense.'

She started to unpack her purchases, pausing on the champagne bottles. The shopkeeper had wrapped them first in white paper, then in a black package with gold print.

'We must drink a toast to your birthday,' she said. 'Just the one. We can save the rest for later.'

'I don't want to be fussed over, you know.'

'Why not?'

'I've never enjoyed it.'

'What nonsense, Lawrence. You adore it. In any case, we shall fix that tonight.'

She chilled the champagne in a silver ice bucket. The kitchen was predictably done out in burnished steel, and it might never have been used. There was a single scratch on the otherwise clean stovetop. I wondered how many hours the poor cleaning staff had spent trying to remove it.

'There is nothing wrong with a little celebration,' Élodie said as she collected together a linen napkin and two tulip-shaped champagne flutes that had diamonds set into their stems. She presented me with the bottle to uncork. I spent a long time unwinding the foil cap. 'Don't be intimidated by it. Ease it off, gently and carefully. You don't want to rush it.'

'You're the expert,' I said, flustered. 'Why don't you do it?'

I seemed to have committed the greatest offence. 'Oh really, Lawrence. Must I spell it out to you?'

'No, I understand.'

But I did not. It was easier to pretend. The cork was lodged tight, and I had difficulty lifting it. But then it came alive, as though I had awakened it, and it shot off of its own accord. It hit me on the forehead, and Élodie laughed.

'Bravo,' she said. 'It has to happen once. Refine your technique, boy. It gets easier each time.'

I could hardly hold the bottle steady as I poured it. Élodie went over to the record player and flicked through the collection of vinyls. She finally settled on a familiar tune. I tried to remember where I had heard it before. It was a light and airy bossa nova that did not suit the cool weather.

'Isn't this the record they played in Biarritz?' I said, transferring the champagne to a silver tray and carrying them over to the sofa.

'Possibly,' Élodie said. 'You have a good memory.'

'How could I forget? You danced to it on the terrace.'

'Ah, yes. You wouldn't join me.'

'I can't dance, remember?'

'I will never hear you say such a silly thing again. Anyone can dance. It is a case of being foolish enough to do so.'

She reclined on the sofa, and through the gap in her fur coat I could see her thigh. It really was as white as the *Olympia*'s. Her stockings were designed with a pattern of black flames that spread up from her shoes. I imagined the garters, binding them to the black lace of her lingerie, and in my imagination I undressed her and left her as naked as Manet's painting.

'You know,' I said. 'You look like *Olympia* when you sit like that.'

'Do I indeed? Well, Lawrence, how could I possibly take that the wrong way?'

'You shouldn't. I meant to say that you look beautiful.'

The telephone rang, and Élodie pulled her coat down to mask her leg.

'Of course this happens as soon as we have sat down to a nice glass of champagne.'

'Won't it be for your husband?'

'Maybe. But it wouldn't make any difference. You are the only one who knows of our separation.'

She picked up the telephone in the reception area. I could not help but swell with pride. She had told me something that nobody else knew.

The record sleeve was lying on the shelf. The front cover showed a woman with a toothy smile and flowing black hair. She could have been Élodie, if not for the eyes. They were filled with joy. The track that was playing was called 'Menina Flor', and the singer's name was María Toledo. I thought back to how Élodie had danced on the terrace, how she had become one with the music. I wished that I could lose myself in such a natural dance.

'That was Bertrand,' she said, having put the receiver down. 'Your shirt is ready, and he says it is the best thing he has ever made. I would believe him, too, if he didn't say that about everything. Come, we must pick it up.' She strode through to the living area, and she judged my appearance. 'You need a haircut, too.'

'I might have to draw the line there.'

'No, I insist. I won't butcher it, but it does need to be neat.'

She headed for the door.

'Hang on,' I said, pursuing her. '*You* won't butcher it?'

'I know how to cut hair, darling. Don't worry. It's better than giving the task to some stranger. You have to know somebody before you can know their haircut.'

I put on my overcoat and scarf. Élodie stopped as she was about to open the door, and she drew up close to me. She took the scarf and reformed the fold, so it pulled in tight against my neck and billowed out like a cravat. Her glassy hand touched my skin. I flinched. It was impossibly cold. We were closer than we had been since that night in Biarritz. She ran the same hand down my back, starting at the shoulder blade. I could hardly feel it through the overcoat, but its presence was enough.

'Come on, boy,' she said. We simply haven't the time for any nonsense.'

I was dazed from the thrill of this contact. At least I could survive on the hope that it might happen again. Her touch was still magnetic, whether I wanted to be attracted to it or not.

19

The low cloud was clearing. A strip of the setting sun was visible as we passed Avenue Montaigne, with its uninterrupted view down to the river. The shoppers on the Champs-Élysées were thinning, and the whole city was entering the mid-afternoon transitional period between work and play. The bars were filling, the wine was flowing, and I was excited to think that I was joining them, that I was going to a real party, and that the night would go on. It would not be lonely, and it would not be spent with a textbook and a cup of tea.

When we arrived, Bertrand came out of his workshop grinning all his mismatched teeth. He shook my hand. This excitement made his body quiver, as though it was going to collapse.

'You, young sir, are my muse,' he said. I wondered if I had misunderstood. 'Come, come through and see it.'

The shirt was draped on a mannequin. Thin stripes alternated between different shades of blue, tapering off into a floral design around the hem. But it was the stippled lining that Bertrand had added to the collar and the cuffs that truly set the piece off. I felt the linen, and concluded that it was neither too soft nor too coarse. Unlike the salmon pink shirt, which hung loose and shapeless, its collar was firm and it was long and slim. It wouldn't hang over my belt or bunch up around my shoulders; I could tell that it would accentuate the muscles in my arms.

'It's fantastic,' I said. 'Absolutely beautiful.'

'It will do wonders for your frame. You see, it is the best cut I have made because it is so slender. Your torso was designed by angels.'

I excused this as a very French thing to say. He insisted that I try it on, and he even went as far as to take pictures of it from different angles. It was a superb cut. It held itself against my body like a second skin. I stood before the mirror, intoxicated by the figure staring back at me. Suddenly the shop assistant's opinion that I could have been a model was not so unbelievable. Élodie came to stand beside me. We were almost on the same plane, despite our variation in height. She held my tie, and she reached around my shoulder to hang it against the shirt, pressing the collar together. She touched my neck and felt my stubble.

'How sublime that is,' she said. 'You have outdone yourself, Monsieur Bertrand.'

'Don't thank me,' he said. 'Thank God for giving that boy his body.'

I wore the shirt out of the shop and we wandered down the Rue du Faubourg Saint-Honoré. Élodie removed the sunglasses at last. Her eyes had recovered some of their old glow. I made the mistake of becoming too conscious of how happy I was. I had wanted to remember this afternoon, to be able to replay it in my imagination—and this made it difficult to enjoy now. I tried to see Élodie's gestures and mannerisms as a photographer would. She lived in the half-light, where she was neither luminous nor invisible.

'He is a dear man,' she said. 'Are you happy?'

'Of course I am.'

'Good.' She stopped on the corner. 'What say we take a stroll through the Tuileries? We have enough time.'

We crossed the Concorde towards the Jeu de Paume. The crêpe vendors were doing good business despite the encroaching dark, and the tourists lined up to ride the Ferris wheel and photograph the city. The buildings across the river were starting to light up, standing out against a velvety backdrop. Not a breath of wind disturbed the delicate air, though it remained cold. I tried to repeat Élodie's work by pulling the scarf tighter around my neck, but only she knew how to fold it properly.

'I'm glad I came today,' I said. 'It's been fun, you know.'

'Days with me aren't always fun. They can be damned unpleasant, too. You should count yourself lucky.'

'I do. And it's easy to imagine. You're happier when I'm around.'

'Do stop it. What did I tell you about saying cheap things? I don't need other people to be content. Nobody does. You, on the other hand, need all the help that you can get.'

'At least I'm not pretending to be someone else.'

'What do you mean?'

I was about to explain myself, but Élodie had gone rigid. I had never seen her so angry with me.

'Nothing,' I spluttered. 'I'm sorry, Élodie. You're right. But I'm worried about you.'

'How very noble of you.' She returned to her old self at once. 'Don't ask me silly things like that until I am drunk. And *please* don't worry about me. You should be worrying about one person right now, because you won't be able to get away with egocentrism when you are older.'

'You pull it off.'

'Me? Ha. I wish it could be that simple.'

She drew out a cigarette. How much of her life had she spent smoking? She had none of the little creases on her upper lip that so many regular smokers had. Nor was there a single hair on her face. Her skin was sleek and pure. It showed none of the work that surely must have gone into it.

Élodie led me into the park, meandering through the pathways until we ended up on a dark stretch of avenue. The naked trees extended to create a spindly tunnel. My breath clouded up before me, and I felt an accompanying shiver.

'This is nice, isn't it?' Élodie said.

'I don't like that word.'

'What? *Nice*? It describes anything and everything.'

'It's saying something else.'

'Good boy, Lawrence. At this rate you will be a true cynic by the time you're thirty.'

'If I'm lucky. Were you always as sarcastic and spiteful as you are now?'

Choosing to ignore this, she made for a park bench. This filled me with hope that she might confess something, anything. We sat together in silence, while I tried to think of a way to prod a single honest word out of her. I wanted to know why she was who she was, why she handled herself so precisely and never showed her true feelings—whatever they were. She and Marcel must have been married for a long time, and it must have hurt her to have it come to an end. I remembered seeing her in the clothes shop last week, and how desperate she sounded when she shouted at the assistant. She may have been in control now, but it was a tenuous grasp.

A lone pigeon perched amongst the blanket of fallen leaves on the verge. He moved his head in nervous spasms, like a lonely old neurotic confronted with something new and unfamiliar. It took him a while to catch sight of us on the bench. When he did, he flew off into the barren canopy of trees. Élodie continued smoking her cigarette. The smoke made her head drift in and out of focus beneath the street lamp.

'That's better,' she said, once she had finished the cigarette and tossed it to the ground. 'Come, we must get indoors.'

'Perhaps we could get a drink somewhere first,' I said. I wanted to delay our return to the apartment for as long as I could. 'I know a place on the other side of the Pont de Solférino.'

'Yes, why not? I could do with a drink.'

An underground passage on the park's edge took us to the bridge, where the arches stretched out gracefully to admit us. It could have been a bridge to heaven, if not for the graffiti scrawled on every railing. Light hung distant in the sky, spilling over the top of the steps. A *clochard* had set up camp in the tunnel's recess, clinging to a bottle in a paper bag. He shouted something at us as we walked past. Élodie paid him no attention, and her stride did not slow.

'Do you ever give them money?' I said.

'There is no point. I once shared a *clafoutis* with a *clochard*. He waited outside our pâtisserie every day, and he would ask for something to eat. I was a little girl. I did not understand.'

'So what happened?'

The Louvre and the Musée d'Orsay, on opposite banks of the river, were swamped by inky shadows. Élodie lit another cigarette and the flickering lighter removed some of the gloom in her face, highlighting the sharp line of her jaw and the hollow in her chin.

'Nothing happened,' she said. 'And I never saw him again.'

There was something oddly tragic about the way that she told this story.

I chose a café by the Assemblée Nationale, which was quieter than most. Élodie ordered a cognac, while I decided to try a Scotch whisky. She was almost impressed.

'What?' I said. 'I need to keep warm somehow.'

'Perfect. Let's see what you make of it.'

We stood at the bar. I caught a glance of myself in the mirror behind the shelves of glassware and was taken aback by the young man in the tailored shirt casually glancing at me, as if asking what business of mine it was to be staring at him.

When the whisky arrived I drank too much of it, and it burnt its way down.

'You didn't run into Ed by chance today, did you?'
I said. 'You arranged to meet him, with me.'

'What makes you think that?'

'I talked to that girl, whoever she is.'

'Ah.' She ran a hand through her hair. 'Well, yes, if you
must know. I thought it would be nice to catch up, and I
knew you would never agree to meet me if Ed was going
to be involved. It turned out to be for the best, did it not?'

'Maybe. But I'm confused—you keep contradicting
yourself. How well do you really know him?'

'As well as I know any of my acquaintances. You might
get the wrong impression, because I happen to get on well
with just about anybody. I have to.'

'Why do you have to?'

'It gives me purpose. We all need purpose.'

She took a mouthful of the cognac, closing her eyes
as she swallowed. Huddled over the bar and clinging onto
her glass, she was as stiff as an old daguerreotype. I wanted
nothing more than to see her react naturally to something,
as she had to the music in Biarritz. My interrogation had
produced the opposite result from what I wanted. Once
again she crawled out of the space I had forced her into,
and she pretended that she had never been there.

'Now,' she said, 'let's have no more of this silliness.
Tell me something about art. The most fascinating thing
you can think of.'

This temptation was difficult to resist. I launched into an explanation of Manet's revolutionary use of brushstrokes to accentuate the surface of the painting. She pretended to be interested, asking all the appropriate questions.

'Keep going, darling,' she said. 'Please. I am intrigued.'

'No, you're not. You want me to distract you.'

'And what's wrong with that? When you are a little older, you will understand what it feels like to be so beautifully distracted.'

When you are a little older. I did not want to be a little older, if this was the hollowed shell that awaited me.

'I do understand,' I said. 'On one level, I do understand. But I don't understand *why*.'

Élodie put her glass down, and she wrapped an arm around me. She ran it down my back as she had earlier, and she breathed into my ear. Her breath was warm. I could feel her.

'Nobody understands why, darling. And nor should we. Hell, I can't think of anything worse than understanding. I would rather be blind. Hey.' She shook me by the shoulder. 'Remind me never to let you have whisky again. It is not your drink.' She moved my glass to the other side of the bar top. 'Now, what were you saying about Manet?'

We had moved into a different space. She could still abandon me, I reminded myself. I wanted to ask her again why she had left me in Biarritz—the real reason—but she would present me with the same response. I went on about Manet, but my voice had become weak. We should have been talking about something else.

'You make it sound terribly dull,' she said. 'It can't be that dire, can it?'

'I thought you were interested?'

'No, more fascinated. Fascinated that anybody would consider taking that subject. Why did you? Was it because that girlfriend of yours was taking it, too? I can imagine the two of you meeting in a tutorial, you not understanding your own charm, going on about Monet and Renoir like you knew what you were talking about. I'm sure nobody else ever talked to her in the same way. I've hit on something, haven't I? You're upset.'

That was an underestimation. My chest rose and fell in a series of gasps.

'Don't go there, Élodie,' I said, trying to keep hold of my composure. 'Please. If your husband is off limits, then so is Sophie.'

'Don't compare the two. She is a distraction, darling. And, unlike Marcel, she is not a bad person. Consider what is really important here. You have to be honest with her.'

'Like you know anything about honesty.'

'Honesty is not as straightforward as telling her the truth. Think about that. And, for God's sake, stop worrying about her. I am sure she has already found another boyfriend. You want to call her now, don't you? Tell her how much you love her so that you don't feel guilty about spending the day with me? In that case, go off and do it. Or come to my party. Whatever you do, don't linger in the middle.'

She checked her watch, which hung limp from her wafer wrist, and downed the last of her cognac.

'We should get going,' she said. 'We must get the rest of the champagne chilled before company starts to arrive.'

The tumbler of whisky was on the bar top, and it was half-full. I took it in one gulp, to wipe the conversation clear from my memory, and to bolster myself for whatever was to come.

20

The apartment had heated up since our departure. Our unfinished glasses of champagne had gone warm, but I finished mine anyway. It did not dance around my mouth as it had earlier. Élodie began to lay the Italian hams on a swirled crystal platter.

'Oh darling, I almost forgot,' she said. 'We need to cut your hair. Take that beautiful shirt off and have a wash in the bathroom.'

The bathroom was hollow, like a polished granite cave, if caves had steel lighting fixtures. There was an egg-shaped marble bath with a metal tap rising from the floor. I knelt by the bath and with the detachable shower head washed my hair. It was so brittle that a lot of it fell out. I used the nearest bottle of shampoo. Soon the whole room was perfumed with the same scent of lavender I remembered from Élodie's hair when we had made love in Biarritz.

I felt Élodie's hand on my back. I started and dropped the shower head. She had removed her coat and her dress. Her breasts were as smooth and round as they were in my memory, and I could have reached out and touched them to remind myself that this was no dream, that they were as perfect as the rest of her figure.

'What are you doing?' I said, not ashamed enough to hide my disbelief. She put a finger to her lips and came up closer to me. Her breast touched mine. It was cold, but I could feel the blood surging through her veins. 'What if the guests come?'

'We have an hour. Now relax. Let me do the work. And get on the floor.'

It was an order, and I obeyed. In her hands she held a pair of silver scissors. I leant over the edge of the bath, and I felt her legs pressed up against my back. They too were cold. I willed myself to trust her, even though I could imagine her taking the sharpened end of the scissor to my throat and letting me bleed into her husband's spotless bathtub.

She was, in fact, gentle, if meticulous. She ran her hands through my hair, then used the shower head to rinse out the residue. When she dropped a towel to my head she grew rough with it. I heard the clink of bangles on her arms, and I felt her skin against my back. She did not speak during this ritual.

'Thank you,' I said once she had finished.

'Not at all. You will like it. Now have a shave and get dressed. And put on that perfume. You smell terrible.'

I had been hoping that she would impose herself a little more, and that I would have to fight her off. I almost asked her to stay. But she picked herself up and left the bathroom. Why had she done that? She knew that I wanted to touch her again.

I admired my new head of hair in the mirror. Élodie had crafted it well. It was short at the sides and thick on top, with a gentle gradation between the two. The perfume lay waiting in its gold packaging. I sprayed it twice around my neck, and then wondered if this was enough. In the end I applied it all over my body. I shaved, and plucked the few remaining hairs between my eyebrows with a set of tweezers. Clothed again in my new shirt and my white trousers, my reflection continued to surprise me.

When I emerged, I saw that Élodie had changed into a brilliant white cocktail dress, adorned with black sequins. The white of her flame stockings melded with the dress. Her hair was held together by an ivory comb. And she had applied a glistening red lipstick. She was clicking around in her high heels, lining up silver trays of canapés.

'You do clean up rather nicely,' she said. 'I work miracles, do I not?'

'You could say that.' I was dazed from our encounter.

It felt as though I had taken a tranquiliser. 'Do you need any help there?'

'No thank you, darling. But good on you for asking. You just drink some more.' She had refilled my glass. Our eyes met, and I could see that there was mischief in hers. I wondered if she had slipped a drug into the drink.

'So what can you tell me about these people?' I asked. 'You know I need all the help I can get.'

'All you need to do is remember everything I have taught you so far. And do make sure that you stay true to yourself.'

'There's a contradiction in that, isn't there?'

'But you know how much of what I do is based on contradiction. And I am doing fine.' Her voice faltered, although I could tell that she was trying to be flippant. 'Anyway, two of them have come over from London. They have a son about your age, but that won't matter because you are nothing like him. The Fanshawes. Arthur used to work in finance, and now he claims to be a consultant, but we all know that he is unemployed. Some of them work with Marcel, some in advertising. The rest are in fashion.'

'Right. And where do you fit in?'

She busied herself by taking the trays through to the reception area. The back of her dress was as low as the one that she had worn in Biarritz, and it tapered off in a silky white knot.

'Select some music, darling,' she said from the other room. 'Nothing too showy. Something that will disappear into the background.'

'I'm no good with music.'

'There's no trick to it. Be discerning.'

I found myself standing before five long shelves of vinyl records. None of them were familiar to me. This was where I needed Ethan, who would at least decide on something and not worry about it being the wrong choice. I ran a finger along the edge of the plastic wrappings, and selected one at random. The sleeve showed a sepia photograph of a well-dressed man with a saxophone at his lips. Did the records belong to Marcel or Élodie? I flicked the vinyl from the sleeve and put it on the turntable. It was a relic from some lost point in history. I was glad that Élodie listened to vinyl. It suited her.

A low-key bass and piano line faded in, and Élodie came through with her glass of champagne.

'Excellent choice,' she said. 'See? It's not so hard when you put your mind to it.'

'Are these your records?' I asked.

'Some of them are. The classical ones belong to Marcel.'

'What if he came back right now, and found the two of us? What would he do?'

'Who? Marcel? He won't. But I like the thought that he might. Don't you? It makes things more exciting.'

'I thought that when you first mentioned him. Now I'm not so sure.'

She put her glass down and placed both hands on my shoulders. 'Darling,' she said. 'Let me worry about Marcel. I can do enough of that for both of us.'

She was so close that I could taste a hint of her breath. It smelled of cigarette ash and alcohol. I wanted to share it. It would have been easy. I could move in one step closer.

The intercom rang and Élodie took her hands off my shoulders.

'Brace yourself, darling,' she said. 'I might have to get drunk.'

She took up her glass again and drank it dry before she went to unlock the door. She held both arms out to balance herself. They were so white that they could have been an extension of the dress. I ran a hand through my hair.

Élodie waited by the door until the knock came. Then she waited several more seconds before opening it, as though she was practising her restraint. I stood out of the way, thinking of how to present myself to the couple who had arrived. He wore a tight tuxedo. There was a prominent vein on his temple, and his expression was pompous. He would not stand still. His shoulders were hunched, and I thought that he must have been nervous. His wife stood removed from him. She had a full face with kind eyes that reminded me of Sophie, except that the lines around her mouth were wrinkled.

'Welcome, welcome,' Élodie said with too much enthusiasm, kissing them both. 'I'm sorry that Marcel couldn't be here tonight. Business took him to New York. But I have found a more than adequate replacement.'

This had to be my cue. I did my best to sidle through to the reception area as though my timing was purely coincidental.

'Lawrence Williams,' I said, presenting a hand to each of them. 'Pleasure to meet you.'

Élodie's face rose in delight at these words. Had I finally adopted the right tone?

'Arthur Fanshawe,' the man said, keeping his hand clasped around mine. He turned to Élodie. 'Good Lord, my dear; where have you been hiding this one?'

'Very good, Arthur,' she said. 'I told you about Lawrence. Don't you remember? I found him, all lost and forlorn, in the train station. I took him to Biarritz, and we had such a fine time.'

'Ah, yes. Now I remember. What a terrific story. What has brought him to this party?'

'He *is* the party. He tells me that he never celebrated his birthday in November, so this is a belated bit of carousal on his behalf.'

'I say, very sensible. How old are you, my man?'

He might have already misplaced my name. Élodie shot me a look.

'Twenty-seven,' I said.

Élodie raised her eyebrows. Less than a minute in, and I had already let her down.

'Oh yes, good,' Fanshawe said, as though the matter of my age was commendable in itself. 'And what do you do with yourself?'

'Really, Arthur,' Élodie said. 'That is the rudest thing you could ever ask in this country. Your first faux pas.'

'If only that were true,' he said. 'I'm sorry for not being more familiar with the intricacies of French etiquette. But nobody here is *really* French, are they?'

'My other guests are. Make sure not to upset them.'

'Wouldn't dream of it.'

They all returned their attention to me, and waited for me to answer the question.

'He is a painter, if you must know,' Élodie said in an impressively offhand manner. 'He does all sorts of things, don't you, Lawrence?'

'Yes, yes I do. I studied at the École des Beaux-Arts, and I had an exhibition at a gallery in the Sixth. It wasn't all that successful, but it's a start.'

'How impressive,' Fanshawe said. 'What sort of paintings are they?'

'Do have a glass of champagne,' Élodie said to the

Fanshawes, before I could take this fabrication any further. 'You haven't seen the place since we redid the main room. Come through, come and see it. We had to be creative with such a small space.'

I struggled to make sense of this. No person in their right mind could describe the room as small. But, then, Élodie was never in her right mind. She poured the champagne in one smooth movement and led the way through to the living area, explaining every detail of the renovation. I finished my champagne and went to pour myself another glass. The night was going to be a long one.

21

The other guests arrived over the next hour. I did my best to participate, although my amateur French made it difficult. I had never grasped the unspoken rules of Parisian conversation. It felt as if I were trapped in an absurd play. Élodie left me to fend for myself after she had introduced me to everyone, recounting our meeting in the process. She was always selective about the details.

Arthur Fanshawe grew very drunk. He tripped and spilled wine over the carpet. Contrary to her words of warning, Élodie remained in a state of tranquillity despite the amount of champagne she'd had. And yet her restraint was more disturbing than Fanshawe's unbridled behaviour. It made me wonder how much of her day she spent intoxicated.

I found myself talking to an Italian interior designer named Armando. His hair stuck up at odd angles, and his thin eyebrows were adorned with piercings. He spoke limited French and no English. The party was livening up, and it was hard to hold a conversation over the clamour. Élodie had changed the music to a raucous swing record, with trumpet solos and tribal rhythms, but nobody was dancing. She was entertaining a group with a long story, and they were listening with rapture. Despite fierce competition, she was by far the best dressed in the room.

'So what do you do?' Armando asked. He had been telling me about his career, and I had understood little of it.

'I'm a painter,' I said. 'Had an exhibition earlier this year and now I'm trying to find inspiration for a new show.'

He nodded along, although he was as confused as me. He was slight of frame and dressed trimly. My shirt was made from a better cut, but he pulled the whole look off with more confidence. His sports jacket fit tight while mine hung limp.

'How do you know Élodie?' I asked.

'I don't,' he said. 'She is the host, yes? My partner knows her. He designed that dress.'

'It is beautiful,' I said. 'So you don't know anybody here either?'

'Some by reputation.'

'And what is Élodie's reputation?'

Armando became uneasy. He must have misunderstood. I repeated the question.

'Her reputation? You would have to ask Sergio. He knows more about her.'

'Sergio is your partner?'

'He's the one talking to her right now.'

I could see that Sergio did not dress with the same restraint that Armando managed. His jacket was made from red velvet, and it had been hung over a low-cut singlet.

'He hasn't told you anything about her?'

'I cannot repeat. I might get some of the details wrong.'

I made a vague excuse to Armando and headed through the press of bodies. A group of well-dressed men had descended around the grand piano, and they were hammering at the keys in time to the music from the stereo. I pushed past two men and a woman, who were taking turns kissing each other. It could have been a performance piece. The wine had been laid out on the kitchen bench and the guests were making the most of it. Élodie caught my eye as I approached. She beckoned me over.

'Darlings,' she said to the fashionistas, in French. 'Here is the star of the show, the boy that I was telling you about.' She wrapped an arm around my middle and presented me to the made-up dolls, one of whom I recognised from a perfume advertisement on the métro.

'This is his first tailored shirt,' Élodie continued. She pushed me into the circle. 'Go on, Lawrence. Do a twirl. Show off.'

I did as I was told, even though this made me feel like a performing monkey. They all laughed, Élodie too. I was doing something wrong.

'This is the boy that you found sleeping in a train station?' one of them said.

'Why yes,' said Élodie as I was about to correct her. 'I have something of a soft spot for such hopeless young causes. He has done well for himself, has he not?'

Élodie began to introduce me. I forgot their names. But when she arrived at Sergio, I manoeuvred myself around to stand next to him. Curiosity had taken over. I wanted to know the truth, whatever it was.

'I hear that you designed Élodie's dress,' I said. He was unhappy to be trapped in my exclusive company.

'I did,' he said. 'You like it?'

'It's beautiful. Do you know Élodie well?'

'Well enough. We met through her husband. He wanted her to have something spectacular that would make his colleagues sick with envy.'

This could have been the same story behind every one of Élodie's dresses. I tried to get an impression of Marcel's tastes from the apartment's furnishings. It was all showy and expensive. The diamonds in the chandelier matched the ones in Élodie's ears.

'Oh yes,' I said. 'What was she doing, in those days?'

'The same as always,' he said, as though it was one

of the first things that I should have known about her. 'Nothing. She has no occupation. Surely you know that.'

'No. I haven't known her very long.'

'Then we shouldn't be talking about her.' He said this without a shade of levity. 'You should ask her about it.'

'Honestly, I have. She doesn't give much away.'

'Then neither do I.' He drank the last of his wine and patted me on the shoulder. 'Sorry, young man, but I must go and fill my glass. I wish you all the best.'

He disappeared into the crowd. It had felt as though some sordid secret was on the edge of his thin lips. Élodie's circle had closed around her.

I was about to pour myself another drink when I felt a hand pat roughly on my back. It was Fanshawe. He was smiling mindlessly, unsteady on his feet. He must have been ostracised by everyone else—I could think of no other reason he would want to talk with me.

'How are you, Arthur?' I asked. 'Good party?'

'I don't know, Lawson.' His voice was a low rumble. 'None of these people speaks the Queen's. I thought that everybody spoke English these days.'

I suspected a number of people did speak English, but simply did not wish to speak it to Fanshawe.

'That girl is something all right,' he said.

I had never thought of Élodie as a girl, although now I thought it was an appropriate description of her.

'She is. Did you meet in London?'

'Who? Élodie? No. I met her through Marcel. Did business with him years ago. I've never seen her in London.'

'So what do you know about her?'

'Not much. Just that she had some sort of a falling out with the husband recently. It's no secret. We all know, but *she* doesn't know that *we* know. That's why Marcel isn't here. They organised this party weeks ago. Something happened in the interim, she isn't wearing a ring.' He narrowed his eyes after he had said this, as though realising that he had made a terrible mistake. 'But I shouldn't be telling you this, Lawson. You ask her about it.'

'I have. She won't tell me anything.'

Fanshawe waggled a finger. 'Tread carefully, Lawson. She is dangerous. You know, in my darkest hours, I have considered her.' He swayed and struggled to regain his balance. 'But I shouldn't be telling you that either. Between us men, you know?'

'Sure.' I wasn't interested in Fanshawe's fixations. I was more intrigued that she attracted this attention in the first place. It had never occurred to me that others might be similarly enchanted by Élodie's familiarity and her ability to light up a room with a word.

I disappeared before Fanshawe could continue. It was dawning on me that this party was open to anybody and everybody. The number of guests had grown to a swell and the wine was running out. Élodie showed no signs of worry. She was holding court as though she were royalty.

The champagne was gone. I put my flute to one side, and tried to find a proper wine glass. There was a liquor cabinet in the living area, and some of the guests had already made their way into it. Large amounts of Highland single malt and cognac had been poured into cut crystal brandy glasses.

I gave up trying to find a clean glass and took a used one from the side table. I filled the glass from a bottle of Pétrus that must have come from the cellar. The label was covered in dust. I checked the vintage: 1971. It was clear now—if it had not been from the outset—that Élodie was about to get herself into a lot of trouble.

I tried to imagine a scenario where we ran off somewhere together, a place like Capri or Corfu, where she would never run into any of her old friends, and where I could finally find out who she really was.

Why was I at this party? There was no purpose for it. Élodie was no less cruel than she had been, and whatever had happened between her and Marcel was neither my business nor something I cared to know. There was something beyond this mess, waiting for me on the other side of town, and it did not involve Élodie.

I prepared to leave. Élodie wanted me to be her clown, and I had played my part. I went to find her and say a final goodbye. Perhaps she would realise how despicably she had behaved, if I made things as curt as possible. But her lustrous head of hair and her silky red lips were nowhere to be seen. She was not in the reception area, or in the kitchen or the living area.

I was about to abandon all hope and leave anyway when I caught a glimpse of her shining sequins over by the front door. She left her glass of champagne on the sideboard. I found her eye, as she was about to step outside and pull the door closed behind her. She gave me an intense stare that lingered for a second before it melted into nothing.

I decided to follow her. But before I could feel my way through the crowd, I heard the crash of breaking glass from behind me, accompanied by a gasp. I turned around to see Fanshawe staggering against the kitchen island. He had dropped the bottle of Pétrus, and it appeared that a shard of the broken glass had lodged in his wife's leg. The gasp ascended to a scream. The blood was running out onto the white tiles. I pushed past the shocked bystanders towards the front door.

22

I took the staircase to the ground floor. The stairwell was narrow, and I stumbled around the tight corners. Élodie was closing the door to the lobby behind her. I called out. She ignored me, and kept walking. I pursued her out onto the street. The steely noises of the party were ringing in my ears.

'Wait,' I said as I caught up with her. 'Where are you going?'

'Away,' she said. 'I've had enough of those people.'

'Can I come with you?'

'You should be up there enjoying yourself, Lawrence. Go back.'

She was on the verge of tears. I could tell she was trying to hide it from me. She stopped walking and held a hand to her forehead. I tried to put my arm around her, but she shrugged me off.

'Why are you leaving your own party?' I asked. 'You'll get in a lot of trouble.'

'I hope so. Marcel will be enraged when he gets in tomorrow morning.'

Her eyes were glassy and large, which made her look like an exotic insect.

'So this party had nothing to do with me,' I said, trying to keep my anger and humiliation contained. 'It was a way of getting back at your husband.'

'Oh darling. You really do paint things so simplistically.'

She had her handbag but not a coat, and she was now shivering. I took my jacket off and hung it over her shoulders.

'Tell me, then,' I said. I wanted to shake the truth out of her.

She started to walk down the street. 'Come along,' she said. 'We don't want to be around when the neighbours call the police.'

She produced another cigarette, and tried to light it without the jacket falling off. I took the lighter and did it for her.

'Look,' she said, 'I only want to enjoy my last night here.'

'That's your definition of enjoyment?'

'I needed to do it. He deserves a shock, after the way he has treated me.'

'How has he treated you?'

'Can't you see that I have no desire to talk about it? The situation is very delicate, and you would not understand any of it.' She raised her eyes to her bright apartment window. 'None of those people wanted to see me. They turned up for Marcel.'

'They are your friends, aren't they?'

'I don't know anymore.' She drew on the cigarette and tried to hide a cough. 'I am nothing without Marcel. He gives me a purpose in life. Nobody else can offer that.'

It was as though her compliment had doubled back on itself.

'So you're going to let that horde destroy his house? And you won't accept any consequences?'

With a scoff, she turned to the stacks of rubbish bags on the curb. They were wet from the snowfall, and beads of precipitation clung to the shiny black plastic.

'I want to go somewhere fabulous,' she said. 'But I want to be alone. You should go home, Lawrence. We've done enough for each other today, haven't we?'

'You're not getting away that easily, Élodie. You have to go back up there. Fanshawe smashed a bottle of wine and embedded broken glass in his wife's leg.'

This news cheered Élodie up. 'Typical Arthur. This is part of the fun. Don't worry so much about it. They deserve whatever they get.'

'Why?'

As soon as I asked the question I understood. She would never tell me what I wanted to know if I asked for it.

'All right,' I said. 'All right. I want you to tell me the truth. And we aren't going anywhere fabulous. We're taking the métro to the Left Bank, and I'm showing you somewhere real. You need some reality.'

'How funny. At least you have learnt something from me.'

'What?'

'You have asserted yourself, at last.' Her voice had become lighter but her expression remained dark. The street lamp illuminated half of her face. 'Very well, darling. This is your birthday treat. Take me anywhere.'

'Just like that?'

'Yes. Take it or leave it.'

I couldn't leave her alone in this state. I reminded myself of the last time I had tried to walk away from her. It would be unfair on both of us if I were to let that happen again. At least there was no swimming pool for her to jump into.

'No more of this indecisiveness, Lawrence,' she said. 'Or I will go somewhere fabulous, on my own, and I will drink myself to oblivion.'

'Fine,' I said. 'Come with me. But you have to tell me the truth.'

'I will make no such promise.'

She set off in the direction of the Champs-Élysées. The traffic sounded faint, despite it being only a few blocks away. The Rue Lord Byron could have been a country lane. The clack of Élodie's heels reverberated around the old buildings. I tried to match it with my own shoes, and failed.

'Did you enjoy yourself?' she asked, as if the thought had just occurred to her.

'I did. They are interesting people.'

'I'm glad you think so.'

'Obviously none of them is as interesting as you. And that isn't necessarily a compliment.'

'But darling, the thing is that I am not half as interesting as you think.'

We rounded a corner to the avenue. The trees were decked with garlands of electric blue lights, and these melded with the neon advertising to create a hypnotic tunnel. Élodie moved in and out of the shadows.

We took the métro to Saint-Germain-des-Prés, and this time Élodie did not give a word of protest. I wanted to ask her more questions—about the party and the Italian fashion designers and Arthur Fanshawe—but I persisted with the belief that I would learn more if I left them unasked. The carriage was quiet and we were able to sit together. A gypsy band came through and asked us for money, and she glowered at them. She was out of place on the métro in her cocktail dress and her glinting jewellery. I waited patiently for her to talk.

'So where are you taking me, silly boy?' she said once we were on the Boulevard Saint-Germain.

'It's a surprise,' I said. 'You like surprises, don't you?'

'Sometimes. So long as it isn't some rat-infested, Irish-theme pub filled with loutish expatriates.'

'What if it was?'

The cafés were empty and preparing to close. Noise came only from the traffic. Young men from the suburbs rode along the boulevard with their windows down and bass up, as though they were on a freeway in Los Angeles.

'Then I would take a taxi over to the Crillon and book myself a room,' she said at last. 'Would you try to stop me?'

'No. I can't stop you.'

'And nor should you. I don't need to be stopped.'

She said this bleakly. It was more of a confession than a defiant statement. I led the way across the road, testing Élodie's method. I walked in front of the oncoming traffic and, miraculously, it stopped. I gave off a passable imitation of her way of walking, gliding past the glaring headlamps as though I had no concern for anything. This time she was the one struggling to catch up.

It was the same bar Ethan had introduced me to, near to the Odéon theatre, with a rusting metal façade that would have been inconspicuous to most people. It was where the Shakespeare and Company bookshop used to be, in the days of Hemingway and Joyce. Decades of posters and advertisements ran across the frontage. Élodie stopped and stared at the bar.

'Oh no,' she said. 'You must be joking. I cannot go in there.'

'This isn't the surprise,' I said. 'Trust me. It will be fun. Isn't that what you always say? Besides, you're all for having new experiences, aren't you?'

'This feels like a very old experience to me.'

She might have been preparing to run. She held her arms out wide and kept shifting her weight from one foot to the other. But then her attention returned to me, as did a sense of engagement and affection.

'All right,' she said. 'But it had better be a damned good surprise.'

I held the door open for her, allowing the noise to seep through to the street. She hesitated before finally she threw up her arms and walked through.

I was glad for the warmth. The bar wasn't much, and Élodie was overdressed. I ordered a carafe of sangria, while she took a corner table beneath theatre posters. *La Gardeuse d'Oies* was the only play that I recognised—I had read it in school. It was illustrated in an old Belle Époque style, with flourishes in the typeface and a dramatic sketch of the scene in which the girl combs her golden hair by the pond.

'This is certainly unique,' Élodie said, on the edge of her seat. 'The sangria had better be good.'

'It's the best.'

'How did you find out about this hovel?'

'My flatmate. You can imagine. He loves bars like this. It's the sort of place where he plays a show.'

'You're fond of him, aren't you?'

'Ethan? We coexist, somehow. He's good company. I would be lonely without him.'

'But he annoys you. He reminds you of the youthful hedonism that you're missing out on.'

'No. I don't compare myself to him anymore. We're too different for that to be fair. Can you imagine me going out every night and sleeping past midday?'

'I am glad you understand that now. But listen to me, because this is important—you probably think that I am going to tell you how crucial it is to be yourself, how much happier that will make you. It is not so straightforward. You need to know yourself first. And sometimes yourself needs to be teased out. You have to let other people do that. Otherwise you never change.'

'Is that what you do?'

'I don't need to. I know who I am.'

The sangria arrived in a ribbed earthenware carafe, with the fruit bobbing on the surface.

'This is rather odd,' Élodie said, as I poured her a glass.

'Sangria in the middle of winter. We can pretend that it's still summer.'

I tried not think of the party, or how long it would be before somebody noticed Élodie's absence. No wonder she lived without a mobile phone. It was unfair for her to leave such a trail of destruction, which everybody else would have to clean up.

'What are you thinking?' I asked. She was far away.

'Somebody should really teach you not to ask those sorts of questions.'

'So I should ignore your example?'

'I never pretended to be a role model.'

'No. You pretended to be everything else.'

'You really shouldn't talk like that. It doesn't suit you.'

I wondered what I had done wrong this time. It was imperative that I did not apologise.

'Tell me what you're thinking,' I said. 'If you don't, then I won't give you the surprise.'

'What if I don't want it?'

'You do.'

'Very well. I am thinking that this place is a terrible student dump, and that you were a fool to bring me here when we could have had more fun somewhere else.'

'Right. Now tell me what you're really thinking.'

'Why would I do that? I never have any real thoughts.'

'You do. I know you do.'

'I have to run away,' she said after a long pause. Her voice was so quiet I had to strain to hear it. 'I have to find something else, somewhere else. Do you understand that? No, you don't. How could you? I have to burn the building down and run away from it. You can't even begin to understand it, Lawrence. You're a child.'

'Why do you have to run away?'

'Because I hate everybody, and they all hate me.' A strand of her hair dangled before her eye. She did not brush it away as she usually would have. 'But I can't talk about it. I only wanted to have one last evening of fun with you, Lawrence.' She looked around, as though she was searching for the missing fun. 'You had to take that away from me, too.'

This made my chest contort a little. I told myself to feel no sympathy for her. I wanted to argue that such pleasure was an illusion, and that she would be better off not seeking it. But this was cruel. I hung my head.

'Sorry, Élodie,' I said. 'You're right. We should be having fun.'

The jukebox stopped. I went over to it.

'Where are you going?' she asked.

'Come with me.'

I searched for the bossa nova track from Biarritz. 'Menina Flor'. Élodie was curious as the first few notes faded in. Then the sax line became prominent.

'Oh Lawrence,' she said. 'What a wonderful idea.'

I held my arms out, inviting her to dance. She responded by touching her body to mine. It was as fragile as I remembered it feeling under my fingers. I tried to lead, but this proved futile. She did not want to be led. Instead I answered her movements and touches. We took up a space in the centre of the bar, and I could feel the eyes of others on me, waiting for me to make a mistake. But for once I had no cause to worry. In some ways I wanted to make a mistake. It no longer mattered if I did.

'This is naughty,' Élodie whispered in my ear. I felt a rush as I pulled her closer. She gave me the energy that I needed. I steered her, and she steered me.

The song came to an end too soon. We broke off, and Élodie threw her head back in wicked laughter, while everybody around us applauded. And then she kissed me. It was almost by accident. Everything slowed down. I closed my eyes. I could see her dancing before me on the terrace in Biarritz, her movements entrancing me. At the same time I could feel her beneath my hands, and I knew that it was no fantasy, that it had all happened, that she was real.

'Come,' Élodie said. She was as sharp and prim as she had always been. 'We must go somewhere more appropriate.'

23

I suggested we go to my apartment for another drink. It made sense, when it was so close. But Élodie refused. She led the way across the Carrefour de l'Odéon. A gentleman might have put his arm around her, but I never thought of this.

'You know, darling,' she said. 'That is the first time I have had any fun in such a horrid place.'

'What an achievement,' I said. 'But now you can't face trying the same thing at my place.'

'No, of course not. You have redeemed yourself, and I need to reward you accordingly.'

'So where are we going?'

'To the hotel next door to your apartment. They tell me that it's the best in this area.'

It was a surprise to hear her mention this hotel, where I had imagined staying with her all those months ago.

'Who tells you that?' I asked.

'Oh, anybody. It is hard to keep up with such a wide circle.'

'I can imagine. Even though you hate all of them.'

We crossed the road to Saint-Sulpice, with the eastern tower of the church standing proud at the end of the street, lighted in soft gold like a stately mirage. I felt for Élodie's hand, and she gave it to me hesitantly. It was cold. I tried to warm it.

The concierge recognised me. He was about to hand me the telephone when Élodie swooped in with the American Express. I offered to pay, but she was insistent, handling the card so that I would not see it. While she talked with the concierge I admired the hotel's velvet cushions and the silk drapery. There was an intricate pattern on one of the chairs, which must have taken somebody a long time to execute. I wanted to examine it for flaws. The mirror above the fireplace showed my reflection, and I was as tall and lean as I had always been, but something was different. I remembered what Élodie had said in Biarritz, and once again I felt as though I was in a Fellini film.

'How funny,' Élodie said. 'We have a room on the fourth floor. Right beside yours.'

We waited for the elevator. I had to ask her now. I no longer cared if she took offence. 'Why are you using somebody else's credit card?'

'Because I am a naughty girl,' she said. 'You like that. If you didn't, then you wouldn't have come to meet me this morning.'

'That's a dubious argument.'

'But it is the truth. And I don't have to explain myself to you, when you don't understand a damned thing.'

'And you like that. If you didn't, you wouldn't have invited me to your party.'

The elevator arrived, and she cut the conversation clean in two by walking in ahead of me.

'I asked for them to send up a bottle of champagne,' she said.

'You never tire of that drink, do you?'

'Why should I? It really is ambrosia.'

'And can the payer afford it?'

'For God's sake, Lawrence. You won't let that drop, will you?'

'No, I won't. Tell me whose money I'm stealing. I have a right to know, surely?'

'We aren't stealing anything. It is Ed's card. He gave it to me when we had dinner last night.'

This caught me by surprise. I had not prepared for the possibility, and as such I found it difficult to accept.

'So that was all a show today?' I said. 'You had already seen him and made plans. Was it his idea you call me?'

'He couldn't give a damn about you. I suggested it.

We agreed that it would be for the best if he gave us a nice day together.'

The hotel room had the same floor plan as my apartment, but it could not have been more different. It was tidier. I liked to imagine that my bed would be as crisp and neatly spread as the one before me, if only I wanted it to be so. But I knew, too, that a room like this would never make a good home. The view out the window was the same, except that there was no film of grime settled over the glass. And the lighting was soft. It illuminated everything that needed to be seen, including Élodie. Her back showed, and under the glow of the standard lamp her skin became smooth and gold again.

'So, how do we finish the nice day?' I said, standing stupidly in the middle of the room.

'You put a bit too much thought into that. We should take it naturally. See what happens. My opinion of you might change as a result.'

I could see her figure in the dress. She removed my jacket and draped it over the bed. As her shoulders flexed, I could see the white scar again. Her hair was tightly bound, and I wanted to take out the comb and let it hang free as it had in Biarritz.

A waiter wheeled the champagne in and presented it on a silver tray. He was about to open it, but Élodie asked him to stop.

'Do the champagne,' she said to me. 'Pop the cork as gently as you can. There is nothing more beautiful.'

She went through to the bathroom, swaying those elegant arms in time to her stride. She left the door half-open. I approached the champagne with some trepidation, convinced that I would get it wrong again. I could feel pressure beneath the cork. The bottle must have been shaken. With intense concentration, I did my best to slide the cork out in a way that would neither be too gentle nor too dramatic. I could tell that it had made the right sound. Élodie applauded from the bathroom.

'Well done, boy,' she called out. 'Now take that approach to everything else.'

I waited for her to emerge in nothing but her lingerie and her gartered stockings. But she kept her dress on, to my surprise. Its black sequins danced under the lights. I handed her a glass of the champagne. I held mine up, and asked what we should drink to this time.

'I have already told you,' she said. 'We should never drink to anything. We are what we are; the drink is what it is. Let us not pretend to anything more.'

'How unlike you,' I said. We clinked our glasses together nonetheless. There was something that I wanted to say to Élodie, but now I was not nearly drunk enough.

'We don't need to do anything,' she said. 'It would be nice, but we don't need to.'

'Fair enough.' I could tell that she wanted me to disagree with her. 'Would you mind if I had a shower to freshen up?'

'You do that. I will wait out here and read the room service menu. It does look fascinating.'

We shared in a moment of amusement. As I was about to turn away, she held me by the arm. Her hands had not warmed up. She rubbed from my wrist to my biceps, as if feeling for something under my skin. Her grip was strong.

'Go, quick,' she said, and released me.

The shower was invigorating. I became aware of my body as I stood naked beneath the hot water, and I no longer felt skinny and weak. My arms were full and my body hair was thick. I could hear her footsteps. She drew back the curtain, and stepped in. I pressed up against her, touching her neck and running my hand down her back. This time I kissed her. I clung to her wet hair while she dug her fingernails into my arms. She was wearing her diamond rings. I wondered if she ever took them off.

There was no undressing to be done. On the bed she forced me to roll over, and she was on top. She teased my chest hair and felt my muscles, and I felt more and more like a man, a man who deserved to be with this woman. She bit my neck, and I told her to stop. But she continued down to my breast, and her teeth closed around my nipple.

I resisted and pushed her off, and we tussled as she

tried to hold me down again. I pinned her to the bed, as I had in Biarritz, and then I put my mouth on her. I could taste her, and I could sense her reaction. I felt her become mine. And then I drew my head up. She lay in the pillows with her hair a mess, a line of sweat on her brow, panting.

This time I built up slowly, and her gasps escalated. Everything was delicate and balanced, and I wanted it to last forever. But we released, and we lay together, and I felt her breath on my face.

'Lawrence,' she whispered.

'What is it?'

'Nothing.'

It was dark. The only light came from the street, where the old buildings were bathed in amber.

'You will get used to it,' she said. 'But it takes time. It took me years.'

I didn't want to think about whether she might have been a porn actress, how many men she might have been with before me. But I did want to think about how real it all was. I hid my face in the pillows. She could not see that I was sad.

'Lawrence, you have to tell me more about yourself,' she said. 'It feels as though I know everything and nothing about you.'

'That's because there is nothing to know.'

'But why are you in Paris? It is not the right place for

a boy like you. Don't tell me that you came here out of some misplaced belief that you would learn culture. Or did you want to find the love of your life in one of those horrid bars?'

'I wanted to be free. I wanted to find out if the Paris in my imagination really existed. There. Does that conform to your stereotype of me?'

'As a matter of fact, it doesn't. I am surprised. Tell me: what were you like at school? You can't have left all that many years ago.'

'Why don't you tell me what you were like at school? I hate to imagine.'

'I did well. I was the top of my year, would you believe?'

'Ha. Is that one of the stories you tell your rich friends, because it sounds so improbable?'

'No. No, I have never told anyone before.' She took a packet of cigarettes from the bedside table. 'You should not jump to such hasty conclusions about people, darling. Now it is your turn to surprise me. I am going to say that you went to some hideous private school, where they teach you how to take accounts and how to buy a Volvo. You resisted that, but you did not succeed. They never gave you the accolades that you deserved. And the boys hated you. They did not wish to talk about the same things as you. And you were shy and awkward. Not to mention lonely. You were too anaemic to play any of their boorish games.

There, you have my stereotype. Prove me wrong.'

I willed myself not to let any tears show, even as I felt a burning sensation behind my eyes. I might as well have been back there.

'You don't know what you're talking about,' I said. 'You know nothing about me. We've known each other for two days.'

'Darling.' She put an arm around my chest, which I tried to throw off, but she was too strong. I pushed my face further into the pillow. I felt her gaze on me. 'I'm sorry, Lawrence. This isn't fair. It's a lie, really.'

'What's a lie?'

'You're a very rare young man,' she said. 'You deserve more, but you have to take it. You can't expect it.'

'Tell me about Marcel,' I said. 'Did you take him?' Her face was grainy in the dark, like an old film. 'Or did he take you?'

'Marcel is not important. He's the easy way out, sheer convenience. And you need to find somebody who matters, Lawrence. Not the easy way out.'

This was true. My tears dried up, and she pressed her naked body to mine, sharing my warmth. She was bound to me. I had wanted her to be bound to me, since the first time that she had left me. But I never imagined the violation that her embrace would bring.

'You asked me about my parents,' I said.

'Did I?'

'In Biarritz. They think that this is something I need to get out of my system. They want me to study law. I can't think of anything worse.'

'Don't be defined by them. What they want is not what you want. What do they think of the girl?'

'Sophie? I don't want to talk about her now.'

'You do. Tell me.'

'They like her. They expected me to find somebody like her.'

'It is possible to surprise everyone. Defy their expectations. Do something bold. Then you can start to define yourself.'

I felt her go to sleep against me. It was hard to say exactly how long we spent lying there. She had drunk an awful lot. We both had. I tried to manoeuvre myself into a more comfortable sleeping position without disturbing her. I wanted to feel her body, but it was also suffocating. Sleep was elusive, even as my body wanted it. I preferred to listen to the figure breathing beside me, whoever she was. Perhaps it was all a dream I was about to wake from. And then there was the question of whether or not I wanted to wake up.

24

I woke to the sound of the street sweepers four floors below, as I always did in Paris. My mouth was parched, and my temporal lobe was throbbing. But I kept my eyes closed, remembering what I could of yesterday. It was a film with several frames missing.

It wouldn't last. I opened my eyes. Élodie was no longer lying beside me. She had upturned the duvet, although the mattress beneath was creased from her body. I closed my eyes again. She had abandoned me, which did seem unoriginal on her part. I had thought that she was incapable of doing the same thing twice. She must have returned to her mad life and I was unlikely to see her again.

I was about to turn on the light and confront my soon-to-be inconsolable self when I saw Élodie sitting in a chair opposite the bed. She was wearing the sequinned dress, even though it was creased and rumpled. She was applying her daily film of make-up—she had been so silent and discreet.

'Good morning, Lawrence,' she said. Her eyes stayed fixed on the pocket mirror. 'How did you sleep?'

I had trouble speaking. My throat was corroded from the different forms of alcohol and cigar smoke. I managed to make an affirming noise, and rubbed my neck in an effort to loosen it.

'Good.' She closed the mirror, careful not to catch her finger, and returned it to her handbag. Her expression was defensive and stony. 'We did have fun yesterday, did we not?'

'Well, yes, we did,' I said. 'Are you leaving already?'

'I have an appointment. Sorry to make you feel cheap, darling.'

'Who is the appointment with?'

Ignoring the question, she moved in front of the mirror, where she touched at her hair so that it resumed its wavy structure. It was drier and more brittle than it had been the previous night.

'It has been nice to see you again, Lawrence,' she said. 'But I'm afraid that I have to go away now. You won't see me again. You understand, don't you?'

I sat up, alert. She couldn't leave me here, alone and naked in this bed while she sauntered off as she pleased.

And while I should have expected this from her, it did nothing to dull the effect.

'No, I don't understand,' I said. 'Why do you have to go? What about your husband? What about his house? Are you going to leave that and run away from it?'

'Of course.'

'You won't accept responsibility for your bad behaviour?'

'You have no idea what constitutes bad behaviour.'

'You are describing yourself there.'

She snorted like a petulant child. Her gaze remained in the mirror, only focussing on herself.

'I have no interest in it,' she said. 'He deserves to do his own cleaning up for once.'

'And where will you run away to?'

'I will never tell you, because you would probably try to follow me there.' She turned away from the mirror and gave that penetrating stare again, the one that said more than she thought. She was making another clinical assessment of me. 'You do look good. Much better than when I met you. Why must you resist it so?'

She came to sit on the edge of the bed. I drew myself up further.

'Why did you insist on spending the day together?' I asked. 'You already knew that it was going to end like this, and you knew how I felt about you.'

'It has nothing to do with me. Do you really regret it? You agreed that it was fun.'

'But you want to have as much destructive fun as you can and leave it for somebody else to clean up.'

'How very perceptive you are, Lawrence.' There was nothing carefree about the way that she said this. It was almost desperate. 'I do like you an awful lot. You are loveable, in a perverse way. But we shouldn't have made love last night. It was a bad idea. I hadn't counted on how personally you would take it.'

'You're right, Élodie,' I said. 'It would be much more mature to dismiss your passion as a casual mistake. But I'm not that stupid.' I tried to imitate her cold stare. 'Who do you think you're fooling? Yourself?'

'Very funny. Can't you see that I simply cannot have you following me? What would you do if I invited you to run away with me? Would you agree to it in a second?'

'I would, if I knew I could stop you from making such a terrible mistake. But you would never invite me. You hate the thought of having anything constant.'

'You have nothing to offer me, Lawrence. But Ed does. That is why I need to run away with him, not you. He knows how to take care of me. He does not judge my behaviour so unfairly.'

The thought of Selvin knowing how to take care of anybody was preposterous. He was no more than a despicable cad of Élodie's curious ilk. Perhaps they did belong together.

She stood up. Resolved to follow her, I got out of bed. She eyed my naked body, betraying nothing.

'Hang on,' I said. 'Where are you going? This is absolute madness. You're running away with Ed Selvin. Where to? New York? London?'

'Why would I go to London of all places?'

'You have a flat there.'

'In London? No, darling, I don't think so.' I wanted to ask her why she had lied, but she continued. 'We're going to Panama, if you must know. That damned silly girl, Vanessa, she is trying to hit him with alimony. And I fear that, whatever Marcel has in store for me, it will be worse. Ed has as little of his life left as I do. You have your whole life ahead of you. Go back to it.'

She was preparing to leave. I took my clothes from the floor and put them on as quickly as I could. She picked up the last of her possessions from the side table, as though it were the greatest chore.

'Don't you dare leave,' I said, pulling the beautiful shirt on in such a hurry that one of the buttons came off. 'You owe me more than that.'

'Perhaps I do. Come downstairs with me. I will go as far as the Pont Neuf with you, and then you must go back. Is that clear?'

She left no room for negotiation. I put on my shoes, while Élodie waited impatiently at the door. I followed her out into the hallway, stretching my jacket as I missed the armhole. She drew up a hand and pushed my collar down.

'It is important to be presentable,' she said. 'No matter what the occasion. Now, darling, I cannot have you dramatising this. It will not do. You knew that I wasn't going to stay with you forever. You thought that I had gone after I left you in Biarritz.'

'And why did you leave me there?'

'Honestly Lawrence, you thought that it was a good idea to give me your number? I am not a floozy you happened to meet, or some constant source of pleasure negotiated on your terms. I wish that I had left you there. But I couldn't go without giving you the time of your life first. You have a better grasp on things now, so you must use it. Don't resist it.'

My headache had worsened. It throbbed like a cancerous growth, pushing against my skull. I felt a convulsing adrenal rush, a cold grip across my chest.

'But why would you run away with a man like Ed Selvin?' I continued. 'He won't take care of you. I can tell that from meeting him. I knew that something was wrong with him when I found out that he produces porn. How long have you known about that for?'

'Such judgement, Lawrence. I have known about that ever since I met him.'

'And you've acted in them. You were never in any crime flicks in the eighties. You were selling your body to him.'

'Stop it, Lawrence. Of course I have been in his films. Does that really surprise you? And, more to the point, who are you to judge what either of us does for a living? When you haven't the faintest idea what you want to do.'

At least it felt as though she had told the truth. I was almost relieved by Élodie's revelation, although it changed nothing. We walked down the staircase.

'Why would you never tell me that?' I said. 'Why did you have to make it a conspiracy?'

'Because I knew how you would react. Ed is a good man. You said so yourself. I think he intimidates you because he has a way forward. You are stagnated. I had to show you that it is possible to do something, if only you want it.'

'He is the last person that I could ever aspire to,' I spat. 'I don't want to be somebody who spends his whole time belittling others, and walking around town with his latest starlet before he tosses her on the scrapheap.'

'And you will never be like that. But you will also never stay as you are right now. I hate to think what a horrible trudge to the grave that would be.'

The lobby was quiet. A young man in uniform was putting out the breakfast dishes. The concierge waved a hand, wishing us a pleasant day. Élodie replied in a way that masked whatever thoughts were prevailing in her fortress. I did not smile or say anything.

It had begun to snow again, out on Rue Saint-Sulpice. Élodie was not shivering, and I didn't give her my jacket this time. I imagined that Ed Selvin would be happy to. It was early, and the traffic was seeping in from the suburbs. A lone moped sped down towards the church. I followed Élodie across the road, jogging to keep up with her.

'Can you at least tell me why you've showered me with these gifts?' I gestured at my new shirt, which was starting to attract the snowflakes.

'Figure that out for yourself. I thought that it was damned obvious.'

'You keep telling yourself that.'

'You have no right to question my decisions when you are so inexperienced. That is your problem. If you would only let others influence you, rather than standing by this determination to be right all the time, then you would learn how to be yourself.'

I did not agree with this, but I realised that to argue the point would only serve to prove her right. Besides this, I sensed that we had only a short time left in each other's company. It was a small point to debate, and yet I could think of no other way to keep her with me. Even now, I needed her help.

'Maybe that is *my problem*,' I said. 'But you have an even bigger problem: you can't control yourself. You claim that I don't know what I want, and yet you have no idea. You do whatever you feel like, and then you wonder why people judge you for it. How long have you been seeing Ed Selvin?'

'That isn't any of your business.'

'So it was a long time. After he discovered you. You've been sleeping together since Biarritz, and Marcel found out about it, and all of your friends guessed it, so now you've decided to rebel against them because that is all you know.'

I made a grab at her arm as we came to the crossing at the Boulevard Saint-Germain. She tried to pull away, but I held it as tightly as I could. Her skin had turned so white that I could see the veins standing out against it, like strands of blue cotton laid out on porcelain.

'Let me go,' she said.

'Not until you tell me the truth. Are you in love with Ed?'

'You have no idea what love is. You read about it in books, for God's sake. I bet your definition comes from the dictionary, doesn't it? I don't need to be in love with somebody for them to be the most important person in my life.'

'So that's what Ed is? I can tell you right now that he isn't in love with you.'

'Oh, and I suppose that you are because we have known each other for all of two days. For your information, I have been seeing Ed periodically for the last ten years, but we have never made love. He is my escape. You are not. Now let me go.'

'No. That isn't true. You've told me things that you would never tell anybody else. I know who you are, and he doesn't.'

'You need to grow up, Lawrence. You already have a little, but you need to go further. Now please, do let's enjoy ourselves while we still can.'

I released my grip. Her glistening red lips trembled.

'So you have made your mind up,' I said.

'Yes.'

'And you wouldn't even consider staying with me?'

'No, darling, I wouldn't. Now may I borrow that jacket? It really is damned freezing.'

I placed the jacket over her shoulders. It suited her. She made it her own.

We continued down the Rue de Buci in silence. The cafés and the boulangerie were opening, and the first customers were beginning to line up. Some of them looked at us with curiosity: I without my coat and shivering, she in her rumpled evening dress and shoes that should have caused her to trip in the snow. Somehow she kept her balance. She did not need my support. I breathed in the artificial scent of pastry, and realised that I was as hungry as a *clochard*. I had eaten nothing since lunch the previous day. Everything had been put on indefinite hold since then.

'Tell me something funny, Lawrence,' she said as we reached the corner of the Rue Dauphine. The Pont Neuf was visible at the end of the street. 'Please. I need to hear something funny.'

'I'm not funny. You know that. I can never measure up to your standards.'

'No. But you can try.'

'I guess going to Panama is funny. You won't have to pretend that it's summer anymore.'

This brought a smile to her lips. She was feeling around for my hand. I considered not giving it to her, but she held it firmly. At any other time I would have felt the energy and affection surging between us. Instead everything was contradictory. She led me down the street in silence, as the snow continued to fall. It was lighter now than it had been. The tranquillity was only disturbed by the passing traffic and the faint sound of construction work a few blocks over.

'You can't deny that we achieved what we set out to,' she said. 'We did have an awful lot of fun. Isn't that enough?'

'Maybe it is. I wouldn't change anything, even if I wanted to.'

'Even my apparent selfishness?'

'Least of all that.'

Her pink cheeks rose up. 'So you really have learnt something. Unless you are trying to placate me.'

'You know me better than that, don't you?'

'I know everything about you. That is why I trust you. It is a shame that you have never trusted me.'

This was undeniable. I could not imagine anybody trusting Élodie Lavelle. Perhaps that was the real difference between Ed Selvin and me. We continued to walk in silence until we reached the end of the street. Some of the tourists were already out, taking photographs of the snow from the bridge and messaging them to their friends.

'All right, Élodie,' I said. I tried to control my voice, even as it faltered. 'I should let you get on your way, wherever you end up. Somehow I don't think it will be Panama.'

'No. But it will be somewhere.'

We stayed with each other on the street corner for what felt like a much shorter time than I knew it to be. I tried to memorise her every detail. But I also knew that I could never preserve Élodie. She embraced me and teetered on her high heels so that she could reach over my shoulder. I ran my hands over her back, imagining the moles and the scar under the jacket.

'I have to do this, Lawrence,' she whispered. 'You know me. I can never stay in one place. And nor can you. You have to keep going.'

I thought that she might have been crying. Her voice cracked. But when she drew back her eyes were as crystal and dry as they had ever been.

She patted me on the shoulder. 'Chin up, darling. You can have fun without me. And, if all else fails, rest assured that you are the only person who ever understood me.'

I was going to tell her the same thing, but I couldn't speak. She was about to take the jacket off, but I shook my head and held a hand up. It was hers now. She smiled and turned to cross the road. Her shoes glided over the cigarette ends and broken glass collected in the gutter. I remained on the street corner and felt my feet go numb. She was about to look back, but she caught herself and sailed across to the other side of the bridge. I waved nonetheless, and told myself that she had seen it. I kept watching until she had disappeared into the crowd of tourists beyond the haze of snowfall.

The numbness spread from my feet to my whole body. Shivering, I walked up the street to a world that had become much smaller. I tried not to think of all the things that I might have said to keep her from making that terrible mistake. But then, I supposed that she had made it a long time ago. Whatever it was. Perhaps I had made the same mistake. For some reason this thought struck me as funny. It was the greatest joke. I laughed to myself all the way to Saint-Sulpice.

25

'Hello?'

'Lawrence. We need to talk.'

'Hi Sophie. How are you? I tried to call yesterday, but you weren't picking up.'

'I know. I'm sorry, but I couldn't talk to you yesterday. Are you doing anything?'

'Not much. What's the matter?'

'Let's be honest—you know as well as I do that this isn't working. I haven't seen you for months. I can't even remember you that well. It's like you're a stranger now. And you don't know when you're coming home.'

'I told you—I'll finish university here, and then I might do some more travel, and I will be home before the end of the year.'

'Yeah. I don't want to wait around for someone who obviously doesn't want to come back.'

'So, what should I do?'

'There is nothing you can do. Lawrence, I'm really sorry, but you missed your chance. I've met someone else.'

'What?'

'You might know him. He went to your school, and now he's interning at a law firm. Don't be upset. I want us to stay friends. But we were never much more than that, were we?'

'I thought you were waiting for me to come home.'

'I was. There's only so much waiting I can do. I don't want you to take this the wrong way. I like you, but we're not right for each other.'

'We're not.'

'You agree? How long have you thought that?'

'It doesn't matter. I'm glad you said it, because I never could have.'

'All right, then. Is there anything else you want to talk about?'

'Not unless you want to. I should go out and make the most of Paris while I'm still here.'

'You should. I'm sorry, Lawrence. This isn't how I wanted it to end. Call me if you need to talk more.'

We said a polite and hurried goodbye. She was keen to get off the phone. I had gone weak, and I collapsed onto the sofa after I had put the receiver down. It was both an outrage and a relief. I had considered the possibility that she might have found somebody else, but I had dismissed it. At least I no longer had to tell her about Élodie. I had gone through every way that I could break the news to her, and I had written several drafts of a letter to her in which I confessed everything. But I had been unable to find the right words. This was not how it was supposed to be. I should have admitted it all to her—not the other way around.

It was the first warm day in March, and I had opened the windows to let the sunshine in. The apartment was as clean as it had ever been. The carpets were vacuumed, and the remaining dust was floating around, caught in the afternoon light. I could have gone to sleep on the sofa, and I buried my face in the cushions, but I remained awake, listening to the car horns and the sound of high heels on the pavement.

I was jolted back to life when a key turned in the door. Ethan came in. He had a shopping bag, producing from it a packet of cigarillos and a bottle of Scotch whisky.

'As you were, professor,' he said as I got up from the sofa. Readings and notes were strewn across the floor around me. 'Drinks are on me this evening. What have you been doing? You look terrible. Not working too hard, I hope.'

'I'm not doing too great. Sophie just called. She's seeing someone else.'

'Oh man, that's rough. So I got here at just the right time?'

He poured two large glasses of the whisky and pulled up a rattan chair so that we were facing each other.

'What happened? Is it anyone I know?'

'Apparently it's someone I know. From school.'

'Ouch.'

'But I don't care. As long as she's happy.'

'So what if she isn't? I wouldn't worry about it. There are other girls in the world, and most of them are on this side of it. Trust me, I know.'

'Sure, Casanova, if you say so.'

'Come out for a drink tonight. Who knows? You might meet a French bombshell who blows your brains out. What's so funny?'

I was unable to restrain myself. I had to tell Ethan about Élodie.

'I've already had a bombshell moment,' I said. 'A few months ago.'

'What?'

'In Biarritz, and then here.'

'Whoa. Are you joking? You went to Biarritz with a girl? What, did she pop your cherry?'

'She did. It's the truth.'

'I don't believe it. Wow, professor, you kept that well hidden. Who is she?'

'See, that's the trouble. I don't know. But it feels as though I've known her forever.'

I went on to explain it all, from the meeting in Hendaye to the hotel in Biarritz to the day in December. My confession lasted long enough for the sky to go dark outside. I left nothing out. It was difficult to tell Ethan about our final morning together. I was still there on the bridge, in that impressionist canvas with the falling snow.

'That's incredible,' he said once I had finished. 'Why didn't you tell me earlier?'

'It's embarrassing.'

'Are you kidding? It's a hell of a story. How old did you say she was?'

'Around forty. She's not the type to let that kind of thing slip.'

'A married woman. And a porn star. This is great. If it wasn't you telling me I'd be certain this is just some fantasy. Do you love her?'

'I don't know. Maybe I do. But I'm never going to see her again. And even if I did, we could never be lovers. Now I don't know what to do without her or Sophie.'

'For Christ's sake, Lawrence. You need to stop putting people in boxes. Think about it. You're free to meet anyone you want now. Marguerite was telling me how hot she thinks you are. Come on, finish that whisky, and then we're having bottles of wine at the place around the corner. I'll get the others to come along. Tell them you need cheering up.'

The next morning, I woke to see an empty whisky glass on my bedside table. The residue sat in a ring around the bottom, and I could smell its sickly perfume. It had been a long night with much drinking and talking and jesting. Ethan had insisted that I was in need of a good time, and his friends had asked me about Sophie and expressed their sympathy, and we had raised a toast to her. Ethan was asleep in the next room. Rather than wasting another day, I decided to go for a walk through the Marais, to see the other side of the city.

I felt the sun on my skin between intervals of cloud, and the faint breeze in my hair. The cherry blossoms were starting to emerge on the Île de la Cité, and the flower market was busy. I stopped to buy a bouquet of white tulips. They would sit well on my writing desk.

I crossed the Pont de l'Arcole to the Place de l'Hôtel de Ville. The tourists were out with their cameras, some of them poring over maps on the café terrace, and the street performers were making the most of the good weather. A living sculpture stood in the middle of the square, and children laughed as they dropped a coin in his box and he danced for them. I could breathe the fresh air, and I could stand up straight and take it all in. This was freedom. This was the Paris of my imagination.

Élodie was there on the corner. It was no illusion this time—I could have recognised her from any distance. Her hair was done more modestly than I remembered. She wore a black woollen coat, which did not become her at all. Gone was the glinting jewellery, although the ring that had so intrigued me was still there in the form of a white mark around her finger. Her skin was cracked, which made the blemishes more conspicuous. She turned in my direction, and I saw that she was not wearing the same film of make-up, either. She was not a porn actress. She was not the trophy wife of a businessman, nor the lover of a seedy American. She was herself. Her natural, unembellished self. Her eyes contained the spark, clearer than it had been. She pretended not to have seen me. But she had.

Without thinking, I started to walk towards her. She must have noticed because within a second she had disappeared around the corner. I ran up to the end of the street, but she could have gone anywhere. I wanted to see her again. But she wasn't walking down the stairs to the métro, nor was she climbing into the taxi on the curb. I stood on the corner of the Rue du Temple, watching for my Élodie.

But she was not my Élodie. Now I could let her go. The clouds had burnt off, and those old buildings were cast into shadows by the raw sunshine. They could have been painted by Renoir or Daumier in this light, and it wouldn't have mattered.

I wanted to linger while I still could. There was a gypsy woman carrying her baby, waiting for somebody to stop and talk to her. A little boy tried to follow his father's impatient stride. A young man with glasses and a scarf was playing a stilted piece on the violin.

And a woman with golden hair and painted nails walked past, pretending to have purpose and that life to her meant nothing more.

Acknowledgements

This book would not have been possible without my agent Michael Gifkins, who has been tireless in his support, and whose efforts have helped immeasurably in bringing it to publication.

I am deeply grateful to everyone at Text Publishing, who have all been enthusiastic about the book from the start. In particular I would like to thank Michael Heyward, both for believing in the novel and for his guidance. Thanks also to my editor Rebecca Starford, and to Jane Novak and Anne Beilby for all their help.

Finally, I wish to thank my family for their constant support and encouragement.